TINA BARTLETT

Scales of Magic

Book Cover by: Tina M.

Illustrations by: Grace Bergeron @ grace.bergeron.art (Instagram).

Edited by: Steve Tuil

First edition

This book was professionally typeset on Reedsy.
Find out more at reedsy.com

Contents

Word Glossary/ Pronunciations v
1 Reading Sucks! 1
2 Figment of My Imagination? 10
3 Junior Year… Not a Great Start 19
4 Late! 28
5 Rules 35
6 Home? 44
7 Home? How? What Happened? 45
8 The Truth? 49
9 Dad's Doing What? 51
10 Landing? 58
11 Astral Projection is a Thing? 60
12 Dad's Journal. 65
13 All Day Pass! 70
14 Something Glowing! 76
15 Today's Events. 84
16 My Drawings Are Real? 91
17 Abandoned Building. 107
18 Knocking! 112
19 Memorpastries! 115
20 Art Knowledge Coming In Hot! 119
21 Ghostly Pale to Black. 122
22 Her History or Mine? 128
23 Drawing or Writing? 135

24 The Messages? 137
25 Random Doorknobs? 140
26 Earth Runts? 145
27 German Is Hard. 150
28 Janice is a What? 153
29 New Wardrobe! 156
30 Small Elf Men Are Mean! 160
31 Swordplay! 165
32 Darkness, My Old Friend. 168
33 Knock Out! 169
34 Doomed! 172
35 Explosion? 175
36 Screams! 179
37 The Truth? 182
38 Legend? 186
39 Call Home! 191
40 Adventure? 195
41 Tree Of Life? 198
42 I...Can't...Breathe... 205
43 The Fight! 208
Epilogue 214
Authors Note 216

Word Glossary/ Pronunciations

Word Glossary/ Pronunciations

Unnatural(s): Un-natural(s). Mythical people in Willorian.

Calix: Cal-ix

Willorian: Will-or-ian. Definition: The world of the Unnaturals.

Nexus: Nex-us. Definition: Portals Unnaturals transport through.

Ripple: A rare mythical passageway that draws in a large amount of magic.

Gaelica: Gal-ica, Character's name, known in Willorian.

Ohixar: Oh-x-ar, a realm in Willorian, known for their two tree's of life.

Memorpastries: Memor-pastries.

Lavina: La-vina, another world in Willorian.

Zweebe: Z-wee-be, (Aidan attempting to pronounce a word.)

Eldrigge: El-drigge, another realm in Willorian.

Travois: Tra-vois. Definition: A-frame structure to drag loads over land.

Creatures:

Yarbras: Yar-brass, Mangy-wolf with two white eyes, with fluid oozing from the creases.

Caral: Cor-als, a rare mythical bird with green eyes.

Aiyana: Ay-ana, a three-eyed, mangy wolf.

Moss Bog: Large troll.

Ondines: Oh-d-e-nes, Unnatural's with lesser fire magic.

Chanticos: Chant-i-cos, Unnatural's who's powers come from volcanoes and hearth fires.

Babonshee: Bab-on-shee, from the Banshee line, alerts for danger.

Illustration drawn by Grace Bergeron

Illustration drawn by Grace Bergeron

1

Reading Sucks!

Two sides, two armies. Warriors fighting on a dusty dirt road. The warriors before me are not regular soldiers. They are mythical creatures— with large wingspans, centaurs wielding swords and shields, giants towering above, strong men on Pegasus horses, and winged lions. With a collision of two worlds, there is fighting for dominance over one another. Each warrior brandishes a sword, shield, club, or bow held high as they yell, charging toward their foes. The clash of metal echoes sparks flying between their blades, and arrows whiz past with a deadly hum.

Outside of the chaos of battle, it is challenging to discern friends from foes and understand the cause for which they fought. The setting sun creates a dust tunnel around the warriors, intensified by weeks of drought, creating a haze around the armies. Echoing in the air rises from their roars and chants, the sound seeming to form a name, though its significance eludes me.

Listening to the battle cries, I hear it— slow at first, then gaining speed.

"A…I…D…A…N! Ai…D…AN! Aidan! AIDAN!"

Everything seems to blur as I feel myself being pulled away, torn from the battlefield.

Suddenly, I find myself in the brightly lit present, sitting on a hard, metal chair with a desk in front of me. My teacher Miss Arkane's voice cuts through the laughter of my classmates as she sternly repeats my name. I glance around the classroom, embarrassment flooding me.

"Thank you for joining us, Aidan," Miss Arkane says, her tone firm as she raises her hand to silence the classroom. "Now that I have your attention, can you pick up where Matthew left off?"

I look down at my textbook, my hand hovering over the page where my pencil scribbles over the words. I'm in the middle of drawing a battle, the one I briefly witnessed. My hand is mid-sketch on the second wing of a massive griffin. Its long, muscular legs are covered in fur, and its talons are long and sharp—sharp enough to slash through bone quickly. A long tail moves against the wind, its thick body covered in rough fur. The griffin has a sharp head and beak, with mighty wings that remind me of angel wings.

I stare at Miss Arkane blankly, "Hmm, sure…What page are we on?"

Laughter erupts once more from my classmates, but Miss Arkane raises her hand to quiet them again.

"We are on page one hundred and fifty, the third paragraph down," she replies, her disbelief evident in her eyes as she settles back in her black leather chair. *I can imagine Miss Arkane wondering how lucky she was to have me as a student. I'm not her favorite student. To be honest, I'm no one's favorite student. I zone out, fail at homework, and struggle to focus during tests. It's not for lack of trying—I spend hours on assignments only to turn in half-blank pages. And tests? Forget about it.*

Looking down at the page, the words start to blur, and the letters disappear before my eyes as if by magic. Taking a deep breath, I attempt to read the section Miss Arkane has indicated.

"The ne...ni.. ggg...oh, the night, waaa... sss. The night was..." I start, a smile forming on my face, proud I am starting so well.

"Stop messing around!" Miss Arkane shouts her words like a slap in the face. I try to calm my nerves as my face floods with heat.

Reading has always been a struggle for me. My teachers tried to help at first, but that all changed when my science teacher accused me of "faking it," claiming I only wanted attention. I tried to explain that I genuinely struggled, that letters would disappear, but no one believed me—or perhaps he made sure they didn't. The truth is, I can read; I just struggle at times. I've always struggled, and I'm still working on it.

"I...I'm trying," I stutter. "I am trying to read the words, I promise," I blurt out. My face is burning with embarrassment and frustration, but Miss Arkane won't have it. Yet again, no one believes me.

"No! You're trying to make a scene! Enough! Collect your things and go to the principal's office. I've had it with you!" She snaps, not bothering to look up at me from the textbook on her desk.

I collect my belongings, feeling the glaring eyes of all my classmates as I head for the door. But before I make my exit, my foot catches the side of the door frame, sending me sprawling onto the floor. *Great!* I tune out their laughter, a skill I've been forced to learn through the years. Picking myself up, I grab my textbook, now filled with drawings, and make my way to the principal's office.

"You're back! What did you do—or not do—this time?" Janice, the receptionist, greets me with a cheerful smile. I love that smile. It's so warm, it makes me feel seen. Obviously, this isn't my first time here.

I've been here *many* times, and Janice knows I struggle with reading. She disagrees with sending me to the principal's office whenever a teacher thinks I'm fooling around instead of trying to learn. We usually talk for a while, and after thirty minutes, she gives me a "missed class note" and sends me on my way. Janice never records it on my files, for which I am eternally grateful.

The rest of the day passes without another incident—a relief in itself. When the bell rings, signaling the end of another suffocating school day, I head home, grateful to have made it through.

Walking down Elmer Street, as I do most days after school, I feel free. I pass the small shops lining the street. Stopping short in front of the local market, Mark's the Spot Market, named after the owner, Mark. This shop used to sell everything from meat, cheese, and bread to fruit and candy, but now it primarily sells fruit, vegetables, and, on occasion, baked goods. I decide to head in to grab a snack. Walking in, I see one shiny red apple and an orange on the shelf. Picking them up, I carry them over to the checkout, planning on giving the apple to my Mom for her evening snack at work, and I will take the orange for a study snack. After a brief hello to the cashier, I give her a dollar, zip the fruit into my backpack, and continue on my way home.

Turning left to walk out of the store and down the sidewalk,

I suddenly realize I must have passed the shortcut to my apartment through the alleyway. I occasionally take this path, even though Mom harshly disapproves. I usually try to reason with her, arguing that it's quicker than going around the buildings and stores, but she never sees my side.

Taking a few steps backward as confusion creases my brows my foo—*No, I did not pass it.* Examining the buildings around me, I feel like an ant looking up and seeing everything tower over it. Recounting the stores on this road, I mentally check off each one: Mark's the Spot Market, It's Sewing Time, Drying Time, and Scrubs Dry Cleaning. Continuing my scan of the sidewalk, I spot BOOM Shop, a comic book store I love to browse through occasionally.

My eyes freeze at the new building between Mark's the Spot Market and BOOM. *What building is this?* Looking at it more closely, I see it's more of a house than a store. *How did they build a new house between two buildings in a single day?* This mystery house looks older than any other building and more than a day old. The bricks are a faded red-orange, almost pale pink. The building's sides have seen some severe weather, with chunks of brick missing along the edges. The front of the house stands behind an old black iron gate guarding its entrance.

Seeing a side door off to the left of the house, I head over to see if I can explore the inside. Squeezing between Mark's the Spot and the house, I climb the first step to the door. I grab hold of the doorknob, rattling it, only to discover it is locked. Peering into the door's windows, I am met with a thin, sticky string to my face and clothes. *Cobwebs. Great.* The excess cobwebs on my face make it clear that the windows haven't been used or cleaned in years. I can barely make out what looks like old curtains hanging inside the windows, resembling a pair in my grandmother's house.

Was this house here yesterday or even this morning? I have no recollection of it. *How could something not be here one moment and then appear the next?* Mentally retracing my steps from yesterday, I remember taking the park path after school and not passing the alley, which explains why I didn't see it yesterday. *But what about this morning?* I shuffle forward, unconvincingly, that the house isn't a figment of my imagination. I know it is physically in front of me when my shoes touch the iron gate.

Placing my hands on the iron rods, I discover they're cold to the touch, sending an icy shiver down my spine and through my veins. I jerk my hands back to keep them from freezing to the bars. "There should be icicles hanging from them," I say aloud to no one. Crouching down, I examine each bar, hoping to see icicles that might explain the coldness.

To my surprise, the rods are free of any icicles or even cobwebs. There are some chipped paint spots around the gate hinges, but from what I can tell, the gate is as old as the house.

Glancing to my right, I see the lock is a butterfly latch. I try to lift it, but it won't budge. That's strange. There's no reason why it won't open. The latch is a simple butterfly latch; it should open with ease. So why won't this one? I try again, with no luck.

I want to kick it open! *Maybe it just needs a little nudge.* I back away and begin to do a roundhouse kick from one of the many "Karate Kids" movies I watched growing up.

My foot strikes the metal, only for it to push me backward, and I fall hard on my butt. OWW! Confused and now sore, I glare at it once more and then decide to let it be *for now.*

Getting up, I glance around for the first time and realize I'm the only one who has taken notice of the new—well, old—house.

I turn to face the market, only to run into Mark, his tall and skinny figure shadowing me from the sun. I decide to see if I'm truly the only one who's noticed.

"Hey, when was that house built?" I ask, pointing to it, only to get a puzzling gaze back at me.

"What house?" Mark asks, in total confusion.

"That one," I point to the house again vigorously. "The one where the alley used to be, right there!" He looks at me wide-eyed, his eyes tracing along the path where my finger is still pointing.

Mark looks between me and where my finger points.

"There's nothing there—just the same dirty alley. Are you feeling okay?" Mark asks me.

"Yes! I'm fine, but you don't see it?" I ask, almost hysterical.

"Calm down, Aidan. I know you love coming up with wild ideas, especially with that imagination of yours, but there's NO house there—just the old back alley. You know your Mom hates it when you take the alley as a shortcut. Best you stay out of it."

"Yeah, I know," I say, trailing off, still puzzled and dropping my arm, tired from pointing hard.

Mark takes my puzzled look as a signal that our conversation has ended. He continues down the street and around the corner. *He can't see the house. Does that mean I'm the only one who can?* Slowly walking away from the house, I take one more look at the house before turning the corner and heading to my apartment building.

—

Later that evening, Mom returned home from her shift at the hospital. I was in the kitchen, finishing dinner—my version of it, at least.

With Mom always working and Dad away, I had to learn to fend for myself in the kitchen, scouring YouTube for tutorials on using our stove and oven without setting the place on fire.

Tonight, I made buttered noodles with boiled chicken smothered in barbecue sauce—the best way to eat it, in my opinion. It might not always be the most glamorous meal, but it's edible and saves Mom time when she gets home, letting her eat, rest, or occasionally help with my homework. I feel guilty when I take away her sleep time, but she insists it's nothing.

Our nightly routine involves dinner and discussing each other's day. Afterward, Mom checks in on my homework, offering assistance where needed. After cleaning up, Mom and I work on an assignment or two then celebrate with dessert. Tonight, though, when the conversation lulls, I seize the opportunity to ask about the mysterious house. She must have noticed it, too, given that the hospital sits a few blocks from it.

"Mom, I have a random question for you."

"What's up, honey?"

"Did you notice a new house between the market and the comic store in the alley?" I ask cautiously, leaving out the part about trying to use it as my shortcut. I know it's a sensitive topic, especially after the incident with the drunk man lurking in the shadows. He approached me, demanding money. Thankfully, Mark was taking out the trash and knocked the guy out with a wooden beam from a past project of his.

She pauses and arrives at the same conclusion as Mark, the

shop owner.

"What new building? You know I don't like you going down that alley! It's dangerous. Someone could try to kidnap you," she says, reaching for me with outstretched arms. She's laughing, but I know she's serious, too.

Groaning inwardly, I press on, "I know, but there is a house there now! Right where the alley starts!" I say.

"I'm sure it was just your imagination, Aidan. Nobody can build a whole house in a day. You've always had a vivid imagination, my creative little storyteller."

"No, Mom, I swear I saw it…" I shout a bit louder than I intended. Mom cuts in, stopping my outburst, "Aidan! Enough! I've had an extremely tiring day, so please focus on your dinner. I want to relax."

Silence fills the room, and we both retreat into our own thoughts. Eventually, Mom breaks the tension by asking, "Do you need help with your homework tonight?"

I can see how exhausted she is. "No, we just have 50 math problems, and I'm about halfway done," I lie, trying to spare her any extra stress. Mom would stay up all night to help me, even if it meant only a few hours of sleep. I didn't want to do that to her.

"Are you sure?" She presses, concern evident in her tired eyes.

"Yeah, all good." I lie once more.

As I clean and load the dishes into the dishwasher, I make a mental note to investigate the mystery house. Why does no one else seem to see it? Why am I the only one who can?

2

Figment of My Imagination?

Throughout the night, I toss and turn, unable to find a comfortable position. The bed is too lumpy, the pillows too flat, and the blankets make me too hot and then too cold. Sleep won't come, no matter how much I wrestle with the bed, the pillows, or the blankets. I lie awake, staring at the ceiling, watching the shadows of the tree outside dance along the walls. As I watch them, I begin thinking back to the house and what could be behind those locked iron gates.

My mind starts drifting to what could be lurking behind those locked doors. Could it be full of games, animals, books, or even horrible things like spiders, snakes, and English exams? I laugh, realizing I must be delusional if I'm imagining hundreds of English exams sprawled about the floor. Or maybe Miss Arkane is sitting in an old chair, grading my assignments, not bothering to read them—just marking failed on each one. I've always believed she was an evil being, perhaps this proves it. A burst of laughter escapes me as I smile. My eyes start to grow heavy, only to snap back open for a moment before sleep finally takes hold.

By the time morning comes, I only gained four hours of sleep as my unconsciousness continues to focus on the House. *I am at the House, attempting to open the gate once more. As my hands touch the metal, I am shocked by a charge of electricity! I yank my hands back, surprised when it slowly creaks open...taking a hesitant step, I pass the threshold when I hear a loud crash as two metal pieces slam together.*

I quickly turn around and watch the lock slam against the metal pole, sealing it shut. I rush over, attempting to pull on the butterfly latch, but the lock holds fast, trapping me inside. I look around and see people passing by, but they pay no attention to me. I jump up and down, waving my arms, and scream for help, but no one hears or sees me. As I scream, the air around me starts to dissipate. I try again, but my voice is cut off as I choke, desperate to breathe. Then, nothing.

I jolt upright in bed. Everything is dark as I struggle to remember my dream. I was dying, unable to catch my breath. I try to grasp for air, but instead, hiccups start. *Well, at least I can breathe now.* I look around and see that it's morning. Light is beginning to shine through the windows—almost 6 a.m. I should get ready for the day ahead.

I slip on my jeans, a graphic T-shirt from the BOOM comic book store, tennis shoes, and grab my backpack. Dashing down the hall, I pick up the orange I bought yesterday and head out the door. Normally, if I leave for school early, I take the chance to walk past the hospital, hoping to see my mom, but not today. Today, I take the sidewalk along the shops near the House.

I arrive at the mystery house and see it standing behind its still-locked iron gates. The windows are dirty and covered, and the worn bricks show their age. My mind races back to the dream I had last night, and I can feel my breath quicken along with my heart rate. Pausing, I breathe and look around the House and the street. No one else notices the building, yet it's just as real to me as the one next to it. After another glance at the House, I decide it's time to head to school. If the House is there again this afternoon, I'll investigate further.

Once I arrive at school, I still have plenty of time before classes start. Soon, the other kids will start arriving from their homes and getting off buses. I pick my usual spot in front of the office windows, drop to the floor, and pull out the one thing that will calm me—my sketch pad. After drawing in my textbook the other day, I copied it into my sketch pad since it would be frowned upon to rip the page out of my textbook. Today, I decide to continue drawing the warriors from the battle. By the time the bell rings, I have drawn the mystery house in the background with the warriors fighting.

The day proceeds as usual, or as normal as it can, but I continue to think about the House, daydreaming about what lies inside.

Why is it there? How long will it stay? Can I touch more than just the gate and the side door? And more important, why am I the only one who can see it? Too many questions are still unanswered.

My teachers, especially Miss Arkane, do not bother calling on me today. Even if they tried to call on me, I would fail to answer due to my mind being elsewhere. After class, I head straight to my locker, avoiding contact with anyone. It's down the hall from my last class and close to the next. Reaching my locker, I begin unlocking it with my combination. Once I hear it click, I push up on the latch and begin to open it, only for it to slam shut. Confused, I redial the combination and open it, only to have it close on its own again!

What is happening? Is there something inside my locker pulling it shut? Unlocking it once more, it finally stays open! A small victory is mine. Scanning the contents, I see I have six books, a water bottle, an old apple—*I should really toss that*—and yesterday's lunch packed in its brown paper bag. *Strange.* I thought I had thrown it in the garbage yesterday when I left school, but maybe I didn't. Shaking my head, I grab what I need and slip it into my backpack. Turning around, I place my hand on the edge of the locker to close it—only for it to slam shut! *What*? My fingers hover where the locker door used to be, relieved they missed getting pinched between it and the locker. Suddenly, a loud sound comes from my right, like metal being slammed, full force. It takes me longer than I realize to process, and I let out a girlish scream! I can feel my cheeks growing red within seconds and embarrassing heat rising from my toes to my head.

My eyes catch something to the right of my shoulder. Slowly, I glance over. A light-skinned girl with bright auburn hair, cascading past her shoulders, stands there. Her head is lowered, hair falling in front of her face, and her body is hunched, as though she is out of breath or injured. She looks to be around my age.

I feel a sense of familiarity with her, but I have never seen her before, and my school is small. If she went here, I would have seen her at some point...right? I want to reach out and touch her, to see if she's real, to check if she's okay. But once I extend my hand, she disappears—gone, vanished without a trace. One moment, she was there, and the next, she's gone! It takes me an extra-long moment, to gather myself. Then, I realize everyone is staring at me, probably because of the scream from a few minutes ago. *It feels like a lifetime ago now.* I try to collect myself, but all I can do is look down at my shoes. The other students around the hall start laughing and pointing at me, wondering why I screamed like a little girl.

"What a loser," says one kid.

"He is always making stuff up," muttered another kid.

A former teacher comes running toward me from down the hall. "I heard a scream. Is everything okay?"

I…I am speechless. What can I say?

"There was…There was a girl…she slammed into my locker, and the metal sounded like it was crushed inward," I start, stammering, still trying to process whatjust happened.

The teacher looks around, searching for the vanishing girl, then stares at me like I've lost my mind. There's no sign of her—or any girl—near my locker. *I bet they are running away right now to avoid being near me.* Coming to my senses, I accept the reality: I must have imagined her—just another thing I've imagined.

"Nothing, I saw a spider," I lie, accepting the laughter from the passing students. The teacher just rolls his eyes and scoffs at my answer.

"This job is more stressful than it needs to be," I hear him mumble as he turns to leave. "Stop making a scene, Aidan," he says under his breath.

Leaning back against my locker, my head hits the metal a little too hard. I replay what just happened, wondering if I imagined it. I pinch my arm to make sure I'm awake and not dreaming. It wouldn't be the first time I've had a nightmare like this, but this one feels too real. The pain from the pinch confirms it: I'm awake, and I did see a girl. She was not a figment of my imagination.

After my girly scream, the day flies by in a blur. Within the hour, the entire school knows about the locker incident and my scream. I can feel the stares and hear the laughter trailing me like a shadow with every step. When the lunch bell finally rings, I am relieved for the escape. At least I have plenty of places to hide if it all gets to be too much.

Entering the lunchroom, I pull the hood of my sweater up, hoping to blend in and avoid questions. about the morning's events. I slide into the hot food line and read the menu hanging from the ceiling.

Chicken Nuggets.......... $4.99
Breadsticks.................$3.99
Hamburger & Fries......$5.50
Go to the House...........$NOW

Wait—What? Shaking my head, I reread the sign. *I've already lost my mind this morning, why not throw on another reason?*

Chicken Nuggets.......... $4.99
Breadsticks.................$3.99
Hamburger & Fries......$5.50
Go to the House...........$NOW

How can that be possible? I take a minute to rub my fists on my eyes and take another look.

Chicken Nuggets.......... $4.99
Breadsticks.................$3.99
Hamburger & Fries......$5.50
Cheeseburger & Fries....$5.99

I know for a fact that I must have been reading it wrong. Right?

—

When the end-of-school bell rings, I sprint out of the building, not caring who I brush past. I run without taking the time to stroll through the park or stop at the hospital to say hi to Mom. I run — well, I'm still not sure where. I hate running and usually do everything to avoid it, but today, I need it. I need to feel the wind hit my face and the burn in my lungs.

The thought of heading straight home crosses my mind, but as my feet start to slow, I see I am running toward home — but mainly to *the* House.

There's a sensation like a pulling force as if I'm tethered to a rope, and the House is pulling me toward it. A moment later, I stand in front of the House. I try the iron gate, already knowing the result — it's still stubbornly locked. Scanning the perimeter of the House, I spot what should be overgrown bushes along the edge of the porch. Instead, they're perfectly manicured. The paint on the House is peeling and a narrow, rusted railing leads up to the stoop. My eyes move to the windows — dirty, with old curtains hanging inside.

My eyes move to the second floor, and that's when I notice it — a change. Between the two windows, there's a new one. When I saw it the first day, I recall that it only had two windows on the second floor. How could a house at least one hundred years old have a new window added? I try to get a closer look at the House, focusing on the new window. To my surprise, it's crystal clear, without a single speck of dirt on the glass. This window looks brand new as if it was recently installed. *But, how is that possible? I should stop asking "how" at this point. Clearly, anything could happen and probably will, especially when magic is at play.*

I can feel someone standing behind me. A chill crawls down my spine, and a tingling sensation spreads through my limbs, freezing me in place.

"Are you lost, boy?" This stranger, a man standing close to six feet tall, thin, and wearing a ball cap, asks me as he peers down at me. I can't decipher if he's asking in a caring or concerning manner. His voice holds an accent my brain can't seem to place.

"No," I say in response, trying to keep our conversation short and my voice from trembling. All the talks Mom and I had about "not talking to strangers" flood my mind.

He follows my gaze.

"I would avoid going down the alley. Some alleys can be dangerous," and with that, the stranger walks away without another word.

Does he know something, or is he just telling me what every adult thinks about New York alleys?

—

A week later, everything seemed to be back to normal. I start my day with breakfast, and then, after getting ready for school, I either visit Mom at work or go to school and hide from everyone until the bell rings. I attend class, daydreaming most of the time and only getting called a few times. By the end of the day, I head to the House and take notice of the House and its three windows on the second floor. I check the gate lock which still holds tight.

Realizing that nothing has changed, I continue on my path home. This past week, nothing new has happened. No random girls have popped in and out of existence, and no new windows have appeared out of nowhere.

Like most weeks, this one has passed by quickly. Just a week ago, the alleyway transformed into a house, complete with a new window on the second floor. The gate still grips the metal tightly, refusing to open. But seeing the House—well, it almost feels comforting now.

—

Today feels like a good day like anything could happen. The air is crisp, and I can tell winter will soon be upon us. I skip down the sidewalk toward the House, but then I stop short, tripping and barely avoiding a face-plant on the concrete. Standing in front of me, I…I can't be seeing this right. Right? There's no house, no sealed tight iron gate, nothing. There is only the creepy, dirty alley back in its original form. There are a few store dumpsters, pop cans, trash lining the edges, and the typical smell of stale alcohol mixed with something questionable lingering in the alley.

The House is gone? GONE! The House disappeared instantly, just like the girl did at school, and vanished without a trace! Wanting to make sure it had utterly disappeared instead of becoming invisible, I burst into a run, expecting to hit the fence and fly over it, only to run straight into the old, empty alley. The building edges, lingering over me, telling me I'm not supposed to be in its alleyway, but I am still in disbelief. It is for sure gone! The House is gone! As if it was never there to begin with.

3

Junior Year... Not a Great Start

Today, I wake up with the dreaded feeling of going to school. Eleventh grade started last week, and things are already in full swing. Every day, I am reminded that I still struggle with reading, especially as my courses become more complex. I'm better at reading, but I still struggle. I stumble when I read aloud and continue to have challenges when studying. Just the thought of reading in front of others sends a shiver down my spine, causing the hairs on my neck to rise and goosebumps to crawl over my skin. *I absolutely hate reading in front of people.*

Over the years, I have learned some study tricks, but I still struggle when it comes to tests. *Don't even get me started on my test anxiety, which has skyrocketed in the last three years.* The only thing keeping my grades above passing is my homework and any extra credit I can get.

My teachers get frustrated when I need extra time to take notes or copy things off the board. They constantly tell me to "use shorter words or sentences, like shorthand," but I have tried that, and by the time I get home to rewrite everything,

I've forgotten what the sentences mean. It leaves me feeling even more frustrated.

Adding gasoline to the fire, my classmates continue to laugh when I stumble on words. Except now they make fun of me on the way to classes, calling me dumb and saying things like, "Have you ever heard of an eleventh grader who doesn't know how to read?" and "He has to be cheating since he fails at reading. How did he make it to the eleventh grade?"

In the past, I was sent to the principal's office for "creating a scene" or "being a problem" in class. Janice, the receptionist, would try to help me learn how to read before sending me back to class.

My Mom worked with me, too, even after her long shifts. She would help by explaining a word I struggled with or showing me some math tricks. But now, she is the head nurse, working overtime weekly, and Dad seems to be coming home less and less, too. Mom always says his job is taking him away.

"Dad got a promotion. He can get more time off if he spends more time on the roads," she would usually tell me before disappearing into her room.

It never made sense to me, but if it means he can come home sooner, then I was all for it. The last time he was home, we stayed up all night telling each other stories while I showed off my sketchbooks. Sometimes, Dad will join in on my sketches. He isn't much of an artist, but he will draw stick figures, and I will draw creatures from my comic books.

Mom, Dad, and I play board games when I'm not showing off my sketchbook. By the end of the game, one or all of us laugh so hard we have tears streaming down our cheeks.

Mom never told me what his job was, and whenever I asked, she shut down the conversation faster than lightning. When I was younger, I would imagine he was a spy or a secret agent working on some top-secret assignment, but now I think he is a truck driver.

In the past, I have overheard them argue, usually about the length of time Dad is gone for work. One night, when I heard them in the kitchen, I tiptoed out of my room and peered around the corner, listening intently, trying not to breathe too loud for fear they would hear me. Since neither filled me in on things, I had to find out information the only way I could.

"Why do you have to go away again? Isn't there anyone else who could work your shifts? You got home two days ago! And now you have to leave again? How long are you going to be gone this time?" I hear my Mom trying to soften her yelling voice at Dad.

She only uses this tone to stifle her anger and avoid waking me.

"I...We need the money! I'm doing this job to keep this apartment and put food on the table! Do you remember how much this place costs and how badly you wanted it?" Dad stammers back at Mom. "My boss knows we need the money, so he keeps offering me more opportunities. Plus, we're one step closer to getting some answers!""Wait, he offers them to you? You've always told me they were required, or you'd be fired. Is...is any of what you've told me over the years true?" She skips over his comment about "one step closer." I make a mental note of it.

Silence is all I could hear. I stepped around the corner, trying to avoid the spots on the floor where the wood creek under my feet. Dad takes a long, deep breath. Finally, with complete exhaustion, he says, "In the beginning, yes, I was required to come in and drive different routes. My boss wasn't happy with my work and threatened to fire me. After that, I kept using those reasons to explain why I had to keep going in, even though he was satisfied with my performance. Whenever I mentioned I could take some time off, you said you wouldn'tbe able to get time off on such short notice."

"I was trying to put food on the table," Mom interjected.

"So am I! We could have afforded to take off ONE day together! With your constant rejection, I took it to mean you had no interest in spending time with me or Aidan, so I decided to continue working! I've been working nonstop to provide enough money to send Aidan to school and keep a roof over his—and YOUR—head. I'm sorry!" Dad says, his arms casting shadows on the wall behind him as he gestures.

Mom is frantic. She starts gesturing with her hands in frustration. Usually, when she starts to get frustrated, she will start to pull at her short dirty blonde hair. After about twenty minutes of hearing them continuously fight back and forth, I headed back to my room.

Sometimes, I would cry, afraid they might divorce, but then again, maybe it would be for the best. Mom could be happy, and Dad could stop worrying about money and finding time to come home. But then I would think about what he mumbled: "Find out the answers" and "One step closer."

—

Waking up before my alarm sounds, I get ready, grab my backpack off my desk, and swing it over my shoulder. I grab a breakfast bar from the kitchen and head out the door. Glancing out of my apartment building's side window onto the street, clouds cover the sky, and rain threatens to fall. The sky is a murky gray, showing no light; only the traffic headlights shine through the fog.

Opening our apartment building's front door, I step off the first step and go directly… into a puddle. *Great! It's a perfect way to start the morning.* Lifting my foot out of the puddle, I shake my shoe, watching each water droplet fly off. With my foot sloshing in my shoe, I continue down the street, passing the market and the dry cleaners. *Do they have a fast dryer? I could throw my tennis shoes inside for a few minutes. Now, that would be magic.*

Six months ago, I started working extra shifts at the market with Mark three days a week after school, depending on my school workload.

I know the market is typically slow when I finish school and usually picks up around five, but Mark insisted I start at 3:30 p.m. He paid less than minimum wage, but it was under the table, which was nice.

Working allows me to buy small things independently without having to bug Mom for money she does not have or is unable to spend on frivolous things. I know she would want to help and give me whatever I needed, but I'm more than happy to work for extra money to spend on things for myself or for her.

Waving to Mark, I see he is hanging a new poster in the window. The graphics on the poster are covered in pumpkins, leaves, and red, orange, and yellow ribbons that stream around the sign. Reading the words to myself, I try to sound out the words.

"Hap…py… Happy…. Fe..fell….. No! Happy Fall. . Fees… Fesst…ival. Happy Fall Festival."

I feel a shiver run down my back as I stumble over the words. My face flushes with embarrassment—an embarrassment only to myself. I forgot that this coming Saturday is the Fall Festival for our small town. I'll have to check if Mom is working and if we can go somewhere to watch the fireworks our town usually puts on. Sometimes, we'd go up to the hospital's roof and watch the fireworks explode above us. A smile spreads across my face as I remember those nights from the past, the warmth and happiness filling me up.

As I keep my gaze on the banner, something else catches my eye. A shimmer in the alley absorbs and reflects the light.

Walking over, away from Mark's shop, my mind drifts back to the mystery house. It vanished three years ago, and I never figured out where it went or why it appeared in the first place. For a month after it vanished, I kept stopping by, my thoughts consumed by it both at home and at school. But one day, I passed the alley without a second thought, no longer hoping to see it again.

Turning to face the alley, I catch a shimmer of silver against the rain-finally starting to fall—pelting down in sheets. Taking a closer look at the glimmering light, I realize it's not the faint glow from passing car headlights. No, this shine is different—like a curtain, suspended in midair, as if someone had spilled a container of sparkles across the passageway.

Walking closer to the shimmer, I lean forward, moving my hand through the shining wall. The light dances over my fingers while I try to close my hand around it, hoping to pull away some of the sparkles and examine them more closely. But with no luck, I pull my empty hand back.Again, *I must be losing my mind or seeing things similar to the old house and the girl.* Even though I am a hundred percent sure I saw both. Shoving my empty hand into my coat pocket, I try to push the thought out of my mind and finish my walk to school.

—

On Tuesday, we turned in an assignment about World War I. We were asked to record information while watching a video during class, then take it home and write a two-page paper on the topic. History is one of my weaker subjects, and unfortunately, there aren't any classes I excel in, though I can muddle through math and history.

Sometimes, it feels as though I'm "dreaming." I'm physically in the location we're studying, and the events unfold before my eyes. I seem to learn better when I can "dream" myself into the location rather than just reading about it. I'd much rather experience the events in my daydreams than read about them. My daydreams are often vivid and incredibly detailed.

When I turned in my assignment on Tuesday, I felt confident in my work for once. Today being Friday, I was *actually* looking forward to receiving my paper. Mr. Rinedenhart —Mr. R for short—starts to pass back papers. Scanning the room, I notice a mix of reactions from other students. Some students are happy, while others are disappointed about their grades. Mr. R. clears his throat before speaking. "I'm disappointed in everyone," he begins. "There were a few decent papers, but overall, I expected better work from eleventh-graders. This is more in line with middle school-level work. You're all graduating next year. Colleges will *not*accept this caliber of work."

Mr. R. stops right in front of my desk, staring at me. I blink rapidly, trying to keep my eyes from watering. He finally breaks the silence and hands me my paper.

When I take it, I noticethere's no letter grade at the top of my assignment. Instead, there is a sticky note attached to the sheet.

"Please redo this assignment. This will be your one and ONLY free do-over. I'm not sure if you were making a joke or not, but I cannot understand this language. FIX THIS!"

Mr. R. continues to stare at me and finally says in a hushed tone, "You have until Monday to turn it in."

I stare blankly at the note, reading it repeatedly. *What is*

Mr. R. talking about? What language is this? I wrote in the only language I know, English. I remove the attached note and gawk at my assignment, completely stunned. This is not my work or handwriting. Examining the paper, the "words"—or perhaps symbols—fill the page. There are dots above lines, and some even resemble cross-hatching. This is not my paper, this has to be someone else's.

Looking around, I noticed that other students were returning to their textbooks or texting their friends. No one seemed to be looking for their missing assignment. I slowly get up and walk over to Mr. R.'s desk.

"Mr. R., I think you returned the wrong assignment to me. Or it might be someone else's." I say quietly.

"Is your name at the top?" he asks without looking up from his book. Looking down, I see my scribbled handwriting spelling out my name in chicken scratch handwriting.

"Yes, but..."

"If it has your name on it, then it is, in fact, your paper." He closes his book, and that is when I see it is not on our syllabus or history textbook. He's reading a book that has nothing to do with our class, yet he yells at us when we do something unrelated to it. How the tables have turned, I think to myself.

"But...This is not mine! Plus, I have no knowledge of this language." I say, my voice increasing in volume. The hairs on the back of my neck stand as I know a few kids have probably looked up from their distractions.

"Well, I cannot help you. If your name is on the top of the paper, then it is, in fact, yours. No one else is missing theirs. Now, please go take your seat."

"But..."

"NOW!"

Turning slowly on my heels, I head back to my seat, staring at the paper. Looking at it more closely, the handwriting is, in fact, not mine. It seems more typed out than written, which is a surprise because Mr. R. had explicitly commanded, "If you type your paper, you will receive a zero. You must learn the history and then express it through your penmanship."

Looking back down at the paper, the lines are almost perfect—too perfect. My own lines are usually wobbly, causing the words to slant or curve, moving up and down. My letters look *drunk* when I write. I distinctly remember it being in my handwriting, and English, when I turned it in.

4

Late!

Breaking the spell of sleep the following day, the sky is still holding onto a dark hue of blue and navy of night. The birds harmonize their morning melody as the sun's rays peak over the window sill. I lay in bed contemplating whether to get up or go back to sleep, when a sudden, sickening feeling starts to rise in my gut. *CRAP! I am late for school. My alarm must not have gone off.* Shooting a glance at my alarm, I see it is blinking "- -: - -." *Did the power go out?*

Jumping out of bed, I reenact the cartoon I used to watch on Saturday mornings—where the character jumps into the air, freezes with their blankets in disarray below them, and shoots straightforward without touching the ground. I run around, searching for whatever clothing I can find. My clothes are strewn about my room. *I should be better at organizing.*

After finding a shirt, sweatshirt, pants, and mismatched socks, I quickly pull each item on and grab my shoes. Clutching my backpack, I start to slip it on, only for it to be propelled back onto the chair, causing my arm to slingshot backward. Squinting down toward my backpack, guided by the faint light coming through the window, I see the backpack is wide open and completely empty. The straps aren't hooked to the back of the chair. My backpack is stuck on the seat.

Momentarily pausing, I have no memory of going to bed last night. I attempt to recall the last thing I worked on—was I drawing? But my mind remains empty.

Shaking my head, I grab the backpack, yanking it upwards, only to fly backward. Regaining my balance, I hold onto the open, empty backpack and push everything from my desk into my backpack. Maybe my mind is in disarray- *like the blankets on my bed*- and that is why my day is starting off rough. Now with my freed backpack, filled with everything I own, I throw on my shoes, trying not to trip on the laces as I race down the hall. Running out to the kitchen, I frantically search for something to eat, throwing open every cupboard and fridge, only to see them stark empty.

I know Mom went grocery shopping yesterday, but even if she didn't, there are usually snacks in the cupboards. *Why is everything empty?*

A bright orange light catches my eye, and I turn slightly toward the counter, where the light reflects.

There is a whole bowl of oranges. Grabbing one, I begin peeling it, the bright scent filling the air. I pop a slice into my mouth, savoring the sweet, citrus burst on my tongue. Oranges always find a way to make my days a little better.

With my orange in one hand and backpack strap in the other, I throw open the door and fly down the stairs. Skipping every few steps here and there to try to save time. *It only saves half a second. It all adds up over time, I tell myself.*

Reaching the first floor, I examine the main floor. There's an eerie feeling lingering in the room, and a hazy fog rests near the ceiling. I see the rows of mailboxes to the left against the wall, a trashcan for people to throw their unwanted mail lies next to the wall, with a clock ticking away. I hear my tennis shoes squeak underneath my feet, echoing their sound. Grabbing the large door handle, I tug on the big apartment door and take the first step outside into…darkness.

I pause before taking another step. It's as if I've entered a room of darkness, blocking out even the faintest sliver of light. *Why is it so dark? It has been at least ten to fifteen minutes. When I woke up, the sky should have already started to lighten.* I rock back on my heel, lifting the foot that was already placed on the front step. Stepping back inside, I let the door close behind me. Glancing at the clock on the mailbox wall, I see the clock reads, "09:57." Wait a second—that's not right. The small hand is pointing to the 57, and the big hand is close to the 9.

I pinch my forearm to ensure I'm awake. I glance back at the clock. Looking again, it reads 57:09.

"What the?" I catch myself saying aloud. It's as if the clock is backwards.

Placing the orange in my sweater pocket, I rub my eyes, thinking I may have misread the clock multiple times. Rechecking the location of the hands, I once again conclude the clock reads "57:09."

I walk over and reach up to where the clock hangs on the wall. Standing on my tiptoes, I stretch my body to grab it, wondering if I can change the time myself or bring it to maintenance to let them know it's broken.

The clock usually rests six feet up on the wall, but today it sits a little higher than eye level, and I'm no more than five-five. When I finally grab hold of it, the curve of the circle presses against my skin, the cool plastic sending a chill through my fingers. I turn the clock, hoping to adjust it myself, only to find that there's no backing. Nothing holds the gears in place, and there's no compartment for batteries. Where a plastic backing should be, there's nothing—just empty space. I can see straight through the glass, down to my tennis shoes. I slowly move my now-shaking finger up to the big hand, and with a single touch, a spark shoots out around me. Jumping back, I drop the clock, causing it to shatter. *CRAP!*

Quickly grabbing the clock, careful not to cut myself on the glass, I place it in the trash near the mailboxes. Then, I decide to head to maintenance and let the workers know what happened. *If I quickly go now, there's less chance of someone else getting hurt by the glass.*

I see that the light is off when I run down to the basement and maintenance office. A dreadful feeling fills my gut, but I decide to knock anyway. When no sound or movement occurs, I jiggle the door knob a couple of times, but it's locked. *Dang it! I could clean up what I can and leave it out of the way.* I tell myself, trying to reassure my mind. Nodding in agreement with myself, I race back up the basement stairwell.

Arriving back on the main level, out of breath, shock floods me. Either my eyes are deceiving me, or something strange is happening The clock is no longer in pieces, shattered on the floor or in the trash. It's back on the wall! *What? How?* Glancing down at the trashcan and the spot on the ground where the clock had fallen initially, I see no shattered glass or broken pieces. The floor is spotless, as if the cleaning company had come through and waxed the floor.

Still, in disbelief, something catches my eye against the wall, blinding me with a single fragment of light. Crouching down, I pat the ground until I feel a piece of broken glass glistening from the light above. Carefully picking it up, I grab hold of the sides of the glass, bringing the fractured glass piece up in front of my face. As I examine it, I wonder if someone placed the clock back on the wall, assuming it fell off. I move the piece up toward the clock, holding it against the newly reformed clock, trying to find where it fits—but there's nowhere for it to go. The glass is all one solid piece, again.

Confusion fills my head. *How, in only a matter of minutes, did it fix itself?*

There is no indication of anyone else being here. I assume it fixed itself, *but how did a clock repair itself when there is a piece of broken glass with nowhere to go? How is any of this possible?* I carefully tucked the piece of glass between some newspapers from the trash and placed it in my pocket. *Today is becoming just as weird as yesterday.*

Suddenly, remembering the main reason I was here, I was also reminded that I was late for school. I returned to the main door, knowing I was now extremely late. Is it even worth showing up today?

Twisting the doorknob in my palm, I open the door. The sky is still holding onto its dark color, not showing any sign of getting lighter. Shrugging my shoulders, I look back at the clock, "57:09," as if no time has passed. I shake my head, trying to clear it from the morning around me as I step out the door, only to lose my balance and tumble forward. I hit the main sidewalk hard, landing on my hands and knees. *OW*!

Stumbling to my feet, trying to wipe off any dirt on my jeans, I feel a headache settling in my left temple as I rub the spot a few times. I look around, and my jaw drops.

"Whoa! I am NOT in Brooklyn anymore." I think, chuckling to myself. I am reminded of Mom's favorite movie, *The Wizard*

of Oz.

I pause for a moment to take in my surroundings, trying to figure out where I am. My vision starts to blur, causing black spots to dance before me. I close my eyes to help keep my balance. When I open them, I'm nearly blinded!

I shut my eyes again and slowly open them, hoping they will adjust to the brightness. The sky is no longer dark black or shades of a stormy sky but now shines a radiant bright blue color. Nearly an eye-piercing blue, I am forced to squint in order to take in its brightness. No buildings surround me. Even the apartment building I was just standing in front of—where I had been moments ago—has vanished. Looking around, I see I'm now in a forest of endless trees. Everything has changed. One minute, I'm standing on the sidewalk where my apartment building used to stand, and the next, I'm in a dense forest with a vivid sky above me.

I have visited all the nearby parks in Brooklyn. Whenever I needed to escape reality or school, I would head to the parks to clear my head, but these woods are unlike any of them.

Looking down, I see my feet have landed on a walking path. This path was once popular, but it has been long since forgotten.

The grass has grown over the old footpath, and new flowers have begun to bloom. I take a moment to look around and figure out where I am. Behind me, where my apartment building used to be, there is now...*nothing*. Correction: there is nothing but trees.

Looking further down the path to the left of where my apartment building used to be, I see a large grove of trees coated in a dark blue blanket. A shroud of dark shade covers the trees, not only above them but around them. As I look closer, I notice something covering each tree's branches, almost resembling a black film.

Turning around, I face the path ahead and see fewer trees scattered around one another. The sky around the trees shines brighter than any sunrise I've ever seen. I take a hesitant step forward, walking toward the bright sky and away from the dark path, deciding that today will not be the day I risk my life.

5

Rules

I walk the path for what feels like hours. I haven't seen anyone or anything for miles,surrounded by an endless expanse of trees. The dusty, overgrown path below my feet kicks up dust every so often. Occasionally, I hear a sound catching me off guard—a whistle coming from the right side of the woods, then sometimes from the left. Not thinking much of it, I shrug it off and continue my walk. It could simply be a bird calling to another.

Growing up, I had few friends, and as a result, I often got picked on by other kids at school. When I started going to the parks alone, some kids tried playing pranks on me. At first, embarrassment and shame overwhelmed me for being scared, but one day, a girl jumped out of the tree above me. She was extremely quiet—I had no clue she was even there. Then, some older boys came around the corner, grabbed my comic book, and started shaking it in my face, playing "keep away." When the girl jumped down, she took one of the boys to the ground. After knocking him down, she tried to punch the other boy holding my comic book, but he ducked before her fist hit his face. What he didn't anticipate was that was when she crouched down on all fours, she swung her right leg out and swept his feet out from under him.

He fell to the ground. Hard! She stood up, grabbed my comic book from the dazed bully and handed it to me with a smile. She was pretty, with short, frizzy, light brown hair.

"Here," she hands me my comic, "is your magazine," she continued.

"Comic book," I replied to her.

"What's the difference?" She asked.

"A magazine is for girls, about fashion or food. A comic book is about superheroes defending people and fighting bad guys. Hey, kinda like what you just did. Thanks for that."

She just laughed in response.

"Can I sit with you and read it?" she asked with a bright smile.

"Sure!" I say, happy to share my comic with someone. "One day, I'm going to be a published comic book author," I told her.

"That's amazing!" She rejoiced.

We sat by the tree that day, talking and reading until twilight approached. I learned that her name was Echo, and she traveled with her Dad, a truck driver—just like mine! Sometimes, I wondered if our dads might know each other.

Echo attends school online, which I was jealous of. She's usually in Brooklyn every few months when her Dad make a delivery here. Over the years, we'd see each other every few months and became great friends. I'dshow her my new artwork and comic book ideas, and she'd tell me about her travels around America.

Sadness weighs on me as I realize I haven't seen or heard from her in over three years.

Walking through the woods, I continue to remind myself that monsters aren't real. Shadows play tricks on my mind , vividly twisting as I travel the path.

Remembering the laughter and snickers of other students,

I know bullies are forever real. Looking around—my heart pounding—I see there are no bullies, no monsters—nothing in the woods trying to scare me. So I press on.

Walking through these unfamiliar woods in an unknown land—possibly even an unknown world—I can't help but feel far from Earth, or at least far from Brooklyn.

I hear it again and stop mid-step as the whistle sounds once more. I distinguish it from a bird's call and a regular whistle. *Back home, when I used to sit under a big oak tree in the park, I would listen to the birds sing.* This whistle has a higher pitch and lingers longer; it's not something typical of nature. My mind begins to wander. Could this be some kind of signal?

Listening more closely, I realize it alternates between a low and high pitch. I pause to scan the trees just off the path, hoping to spot anyone hiding there. With no luck, I keep moving, walking past the sound and toward the clearing up ahead."

—

My stomach grumbles with hunger. I wish I had more than the orange I had intended to eat earlier. I had searched my pocket frantically, turning it inside out, only to realize that I must have dropped it when I tumbled down the concrete stairs. The thought of food makes my stomach rumble again.

"Man, I *wish* I had something to eat," I say out loud.

Catching myself, I stop speaking, not realizing I had said the words aloud until I hear a sharp, pinging sound coming from the forest. Looking toward the trees, I spot different types of fruit growing from their branches. Within a minute, there are at least fifty bright red and shiny apples, perfect green pears, and vibrant purple grapes, all dangling off each tree's branches. I reach up to grab a bunch of grapes, amused,—it's not every day you find a tree that can grow two to three different fruits simultaneously. Suddenly, something catches my eye a shadow moving quickly between the trees. It's moving swiftly and quietly, as though its owner knows the danger of this place. The shadow grows closer and closer. *What lurks behind the trees?* I can't tell what it is until something shoots straight toward me. I hear it moving through the air at top speed but can't make out the object. *What, what is it?* BANG!

It hits me—wait! No, not me. It hits the fruit I'm holding, just inches from my face!

The object, a small, jagged rock, hits the grape stem, sending the fruit flying out of my hand. I watch as each grape falls to the ground, rolling around in the dirt. Each grape still looks as clean and beautiful as it did when it was hanging from the stem. Reaching down, I go to grab one of the shiny fruits when a figure jumps out of nowhere and kicks the grapes away from my hand. Their foot strikes the fruit like a soccer ball, mere inches from my sprawled-out fingers.

"Hey!" I shout. Looking up, I see it's a young girl, maybe around my age.

"STOP!" she yells. *I know that voice, but how?*

"What do you mean, stop?" I shout back at her.

"DON'T EVEN THINK ABOUT EATING THAT!" *Is that Echo? No... no... Maybe? Can it be?*

"But, I'm hungry, and I wi-" Her hand slams against my mouth before I can finish my sentence.

"Shhh. Do NOT say that word." *Yup! That's Echo, with her snarky comments, still holding* her hand over my mouth.

I try to speak, but it comes out as a mumble.

"Are you going to say that word?" She asks me as she glares at me with a serious look.

In this moment, I see her. I see her bright blue eyes and dirty brown hair, now grown out, long past her shoulders.

I shake my head, murmuring "I promise I will not say that word." She nods and removes her hand.

A rush of cool air hits my skin where her hand was. I try looking at her, but she's standing in the shadow of the trees, making it hard to see her clearly.

"Okay," she says slowly, as though she's hesitating. "We need to get out of these woods." She starts walking forward.

"Why? Wait—Echo?"

"Yes? Why are we still standing here?" She says, exasperated.

"Don't you remember? I haven't seen you in years and you show up now, out of the blue?" I ask, in complete shock.

"Okay," she pauses. "We need to catch up on a few things, but first, we need to get out of here—clearly, since you're unaware of where we are." she chuckles. "I wi…" she stops herself. "See? I almost did it. I'd hoped to find you earlier. Who knows what you would've said before I found you? Do you have any idea what kind of trouble you could've gotten into? It can get dangerous in these woods, real quick."

"What the—" I start to say, but she cuts me off.

"Stop! You are not allowed to speak. Not until I've gone through the rules for venturing through these woods."

I stare at her, shocked. Really, I can't believe she's here. And to be honest, I don't recall her being this bossy before.

"Okay," she starts again after taking a deep breath. "We're going to continue down this path, and when it gets dark enough, we'll use a flashlight to help us see."

"Why…?" I begin to ask, but catch myself before finishing.

I can feel her shooting me a look. The bright blue sky is getting darker, starting to resemble the dark woods behind me earlier. *I wonder if I somehow got turned around and went in the wrong direction.*

"Please, just stop talking. I'm sorry, but I'll explain everything along the way. We can't afford for you to say the wrong thing, and I need to fix a bigger problem than the one I found you in. Nod if you understand."

I nod slowly at first, then speed it up. I'm not sure if Echo can see me, but I hope she can since she won't let me speak. She takes a deep breath in and lets it out.

We return to the path and set off. I feel the wind travel through my sweatshirt, sending a shiver down my spine. *I want to comment on it but decide against it. For the entire journey, I had no one to talk to, and when I spoke a single word, it felt like I had no control over my actions once something popped into my head. In that moment, it was the need to find food, but when Echo stopped me and demanded I not speak, I wondered if she knew I had zero control over what I said.*

"...Me?" Her words pull me from my thoughts. I grunt, remembering not to speak.

"Ugh, I asked if you heard me." She pokes my shoulder hard with her index finger. I shake my head in response. I'd bet anything she just rolled her eyes at me. If only I could see her face.

"What I was saying when you were daydreaming over there," she rolls her eyes, "you need to minimize your words in these woods since you're not trained. I can speak because I can fight the urge to say the wrong words." She takes a deep breath, briefly closes her eyes,

then, with a flourish as her eyelashes flutter open, she starts again.

"These woods are called the *Wishing Trees.* The Wishing

Trees are scattered throughout, but no one knows which ones they are. Many have searched and failed. The reason you have to be trained to come through here is because many have tried and failed to find their way out, and if they do make it..." She trails off, thinking silently for a moment, then continues, "They come back different. Along with the Wishing Trees, some trees contain malevolent magic. If trees could be villainous, these trees would be the definition of it.

We don't *exactly* know how the magic works, but once someone eats the fruit or gets whatever they *asked* for, the tree will shake its branches, releasing pollen that makes the person feel sleepy. Usually, they don't survive in the forest. They stumble and lie beneath another tree, and after that, the person vanishes, going missing." She pauses as if she's fighting back tears. Shaking her head, she continues, "There are stringent rules you must remember when walking through these woods. Most people who come through here are driving or racing through, not walking leisurely like you. The longer you stay the stronger the urge to say the words that can get you into trouble. And if you're not careful, you can get lost and never make it out."

She clears her throat.

"Shockingly, you're still here, I was able to find you, and you didn't get sucked into a tree." She laughs to herself. My eyes enlarge. *Did she say, "sucked into a tree?"* She pauses for a few moments, then starts up again.

"I bet you have many questions, and once we're out of the woods, I will answer them, but not yet. The rules—there are ten of them. I hope you have a good memory, or at least enough time to learn and memorize them before you come back here. Everyone has to have them memorized before they can leave the school."

At the word "*school*," I shot up to look at her. *Great. I left one school and went straight into another—just my luck.*

"Hey, Aidan, you need to listen!" She taps my shoulder. *So, she does remember me!* I nod rapidly, telling her that I'm here and concentrating.

"Okay, here we go." She takes a deep breath and begins:

"1. They're called the Wishing Trees because they will grant you *anything* you *w-i-s-h* for. There are no accidents. Even if you say the "w-i-s-h." she spells the word in a low whisper, "it will be granted."

2. Go in and get out.

The longer you stay in the woods, the stronger the tree's magic will pull on you. They want to take all the pure magic and suck you dry, literally.

3. Always go in with others.

We're safer in numbers. We help each other through the woods.

4. Bring food.

For the exact reason, I saved you from.

5. Always bring gear.

Whether it's survival gear, rain gear, sun protection, or anything else, if you get caught in the woods on a scorching hot day and *accidentally ask* for rain, it will come—but it'll be acidic, and it'll feel like your skin is melting off. That is how evil magic works. Like the food—if you had eaten it—it could give you an upset stomach or send you in excruciating pain. It would feel like your insides were spilling out.

6. You must know how to throw a knife.

We'll teach you, but it's a skill you'll need to learn. You never know when you'll need to throw a knife to protect yourself or others. You'll also learn how to fight, but that's a lesson for another day.

7. Learn call signals.

There are different whistles, cues, and ways to communicate without actually saying words. I saw you earlier and tried signaling to you. Clearly, you don't know any of the signals. Don't worry, though— you'll learn.

8. Learn your power.

Training will teach you that. Everyone has different powers and types of magic. You'll need to harness yours and learn how to use it. Once you master it, you'll learn how to use it against your enemies.

9. Bring backup power/magic.

In these woods, you'll either drain your power by defending yourself, or the woods will find a way to drain it for you.

If you want additional power or magic to help you find your way out, you're in for a challenge. Paths like this one are rare, and the woods constantly change, making it harder each time you venture in.

10. Communication is KEY!

Straight forward, tell people where you're going."

As soon as the last words left her lips, we walked into an opening in the trees. The light was blindingly bright. I raised my hand above my eyes to shield them. It was as if someone had flipped a switch and turned on every light at once. On my left, I heard Echo gulp and exclaim, "Crap!" as she came to a sudden halt. My eyes were still blinded, and I had no idea what was happening when I heard it.

"ECHO!" A booming voice reverberates in my ears. "Where did you run off to?"

6

Home?

Before Echo can say another word, I'm yanked out of the woods, ripped from the world I was just in, no longer standing beside her. Everything around me whirls past as though I'm being tossed around in a tornado. I close my eyes and take a deep breath, trying not to puke.

After what feels like minutes, the spinning finally stops. Slowly, I open my eyes and reach my hands out, feeling along the walls. My hand grazes something that feels like a light switch. I grab it and flick it up. The light takes a moment to warm up, and to my surprise, I see the clock, the mailboxes, and the stairway behind me. I whip around, taking everything in—including the large apartment building door in front of me. I'm back home.

7

Home? How? What Happened?

I sprint out of the building like I did this morning, only to open the door and find a bright, sunny day with no clouds in the sky—much different from before. I still have no idea where I went, but if I have the chance to go back, I'll have to remember to ask where I was.

Looking around, I hear birds chirping and people walking about. The last time I opened this door, not a soul was in sight. The sky and area before me were pitch black.

Squinting against the sunlight, I notice there are more vehicles on the side of the road than usual. Usually, there are more vehicles if someone's hosting a party or event, but on a weekday everyone is busy with work. One vehicle catches my eye. I raise my hand above my eyes to block the sun, trying to make out the logo. Frustrated that my eyes and brain are not working together, I head out the front door and down the steps for the second time today. As I head towards the car, I wonder if I'll get sucked into a different world again. But once I pass the second step, I'm back for good, at least for now.

The car is now in front of me. The logo features two

figures, resembling the girl and boy shapes on a bathroom sign, surrounded by circular patterns and a world in the background. Across the front of the circles and Earth is a word. For once, I can read it on my first try. "Riverstones." I repeat the word, both in my head and aloud, feeling a sense of pride for being able to read it. But then, with barely a breath, my world is rocked again!

Looking around, I see I'm in front of a vast lake with trees surrounding it. There are two groups of people—both males and females—on each side of the lake. They range in age from about thirteen to nearly seventy. They begin talking to one another, but I'm too far away to make out their words. Deciding to get closer, I try to move my feet, only to find them stuck firmly in the mud underneath my shoes. Unable to move, I can't get close enough to hear what they're saying.There's magic here. I can feel it. The air is thick—almost sickeningly so—and a sudden rush of energy races through the trees, gathering in the center of the lake. I can feel it bouncing off everything: the trees, the people, the water, the stones...even myself. Wait—stones? Nineteen glowing, oval-shaped items are floating in the air.

Movement catches my attention, glowing brightly just below my face. Looking down, I see an object in my hands. It's oval shape, similar to the ones by the lake with the people. The object looks like a flat skipping stone. I try to turn it over with my other hand, but to my surprise, I can't move it. My free hand is stuck.

The vision—or what I have been calling them—changes rapidly, as though I'm being pushed through time once again.

"Do you have it?" A high-pitched voice behind me calls out.

"Yes! We have to protect it.... and the house." Says another voice. It sounds like it's coming from me, but it's not my voice. It's that of a boy, probably a few years older than I am.

"Good. We have to go—and we have to go now!" says the high-pitched voice.

"What if they find them all... or the house after we hide them?"

"Then they will be in danger. They'll all be in danger. We are hiding the stones and the house to protect the Unnatural's future. If the house or stones are found, whoever finds them will possess their magic, and war will break out...or the world will burn!"

"Is there a certain number of stones one would have to find for the prophecy to come true?"

"Yes. Someone would have to find *all* the stones and the house. Though the house has been hidden so well, no one should be able to find it. Only one person knew its location, and he's since passed."

"And if all of these are found and brought to the house's location, then the war of all wars will be set into motion?"

"Correct, no one will be able to handle its power. War will break out. That's why we are in charge of the stones and the need to hide them. We're the only two who know their locations, and if anything were to happen to us, the secret locations will die with us."

"Well, good. Hopefully, no one will ever possess that amount of magic. Who knows what would be left of our world and Earth if those were all found? Magic would become unstable."

"Exactly! Now, *please* help me figure out the last few hiding spells."

With a static crackle, I'm pulled back into reality. I'm still on the sidewalk near the car with the logo on it, but now there's an unfamiliar weight in my right hand. Looking down, I see a stone. Is this the one from my vision? Or was it all a dream? Whatever it was, the stone is in my hand now.

"HEY! Kid!" a shout comes from behind me. I see you trying to break into that government car. I've already called the cops. They're coming and will be here any minute. PUT the rock down!"

Startled, I look up to see a woman,probably about my mother's age, dressed in fancy clothes and holding her cell phone to her ear. She's still talking to whoever is on the other end—likely the police.

Knowing I only have minutes to decide, I quickly grasp the stone and race back into my apartment building and up the stairs to my apartment I fling open the door, letting out a sigh of relief. I close my eyes for a moment, relishing the quiet. It lasts only one second.

8

The Truth?

"AIDAN! Where have you been?" A voice rang out—my mother's voice, sharp and angry. *Oh no.*

My eyes snap open, and I see my mom standing in the kitchen. Glancing at the clock, I realize it's the middle of the day. Why is she home? Moving my eyes back her, I notice two other people standing in the kitchen near the counter: a woman and a man. They're both dressed in suits and holding briefcases. Papers are scattered across the counter.

I freeze, unsure of what to say or do. I'mnot prepared for what Mom does next. She runs over at full speed, *which is shocking since she was only a few feet from me to begin with,* and hugs me. It's the kind of hug you give a family member who's been gone for a long time—the kind that makes you forget all your troubles and feel the warmth of their arms around you. That'sthe type of hug my mom is giving me.

"Mom," I start, "Mom, are you okay? Is everything okay?"

"Where have you been?" She talks over my questions, and I can tell she is scared. The worry lines on her face are more pronounced.

"What do you mean?"

I'm trying not to think about the fact that I was just in another world, saw Echo again, and learned about another world and trees that can trap you and kill you. Then there was the vision about a house—I'm assuming it's the mystery house, the one no one else can see but me. But I could be wrong.

I slowly move the stone behind my back and into my back pocket, praying I hid it before she noticed.

"You have been missing for three days! I have been worried sick." She pauses as though she's contemplating saying something else, then continues.

"At first, I hate to admit it, but I picked up an extra shift at the hospital the first day, so I stayed there overnight. On the second day, I got a call from your school asking about your whereabouts. I raced home, fearing something might have happened to you. Where were you?!" She practically shouts the last few words.

Three days? How? It only felt like hours. That could explain why the weather was significantly different when I returned, but still, three days? Can I tell her where I went and who I met? Would she believe me? Wait a second, who are the other people in the room?

"Mom, I am okay, but who are they?" I ask her instead. Avoiding her original question.

"Honey," she exhales deeply, probably releasing a breath she's been holding in for the past three days, "We need to talk."

9

Dad's Doing What?

Mom ended up telling me everything. And I mean everything. It took her a minute to figure out how to start, but she told me she and my Dad adopted me. They found me abandoned in a basket at the hospital. At the time, she was a certified nursing assistant (CNA) and was the one who found me. She took care of me there, and when I was healthy enough, my parents brought me home. There was no record of my birth, and no other living or deceased relatives could be traced to my DNA. In fact, my DNA records came up invalid. I was a mystery. My parents had struggled with infertility, and after working with a social worker, they were told that, since there was no record of me or my family, they could fill out the adoption papers and take me home.

One day, when Mom was working, my Dad was at home watching me. I was on Dad's lap as he lightly tossed me up into the air, and then the next thing he knew, I was gone! Mom remarked that he had searched the house with no luck. After hours of panic and worry, I suddenly reappeared as though nothing had happened. The only difference was the flat stone held in my hand, which seemed to glisten in every kind of light—even in complete darkness. Dad was shocked and horrified, fearing I had gotten involved in something dangerous wherever I'd been. He immediately called Mom, and she rushed home. Dad was trying to explain what had happened.

Mom wasn't thrilled about me being gone for a few hours without anyone knowing. Dad had no answers, and she wasn't having it. With her curious, science-driven mind, she started digging through hospital records to see if there were any other cases like mine—young children abandoned, with no relatives or records in the system. While there were no other living children like me, she did find one odd case: a young girl who had passed through the system twelve years ago. As Mom flipped through the file, she discovered the girl had died from "unknown causes." But what really caught her attention was the logo on the file—a pair of children, a boy and a girl, surrounded by circles with the Earth in the background. The words "Riverstones" were written across the image. After what seemed like endless research, she managed to track down the company and make contact with them.

It turns out, Riverstones is a company that works with children,—those who were abandoned or placed into the foster care system for unknown reasons. To the outside world, they care for these children until they can find good homes. That's the public face of the company. But behind the logo is magic. Riverstones is a convert organization that searches for Unnatural children—those born with magic. The company either watches them from a distance, or if they sense the child is in danger, they intervene by bringing them to another world. I learned that this other world is called Willorian, which translates to the Nation of Wild Ones.

Willorian exists in another realm. While it's similar to Earth in many ways, it is a world that is deeply intertwined with magic, where the land and its people are connected through mystical forces.

As Mom understood it, many years ago, a dispute erupted between the Unnaturals and the Creatures of Willorian. The conflict stemmed from one side trying to gain and control more power than they could physically contain. A group of Unnaturals banded together to challenge the current power structure. When the War of all Wars broke out, a council of Elders took charge and divided the power into fallen dragon scales.

Dragons were once known to harness magic hundreds of years ago, but they have since ceased to exist. Some Elders, however, still had access to fallen dragon scales, which retained the ability to harness magic. Along with these scales, the center of all magic lies in a sacred place—the original source of magic: a house. This house provided shelter and protection from evil, as well as refuge for those at risk of exposure, such as those who were unable to control their powers or possessed rare abilities.

The house possessed the knowledge to discern the difference, almost as if it were alive itself. It is said that the Elders infused all of their magic into hiding the scales in the deepest, most terrifying parts of the world, places where no one could or would venture to. Some scales are even invisible, while the house itself was sent into another realm. No one knows its location, nor how the Elders intend to keep it hidden.

The scales still harness magic, and if someone were to find one, all they would have to do is break it in half to "absorb" the magic within. The catch, however, is no one knows what kind of magic resides in each scale. The person choosing to break and harness the power would essentially be gambling with their life. The magic could range from a lesser power to something incredibly dangerous.

"Now," Mom takes a deep breath, "when you failed to come home, I got worried. I remember you mentioning a house that showed up one day and disappeared again. I feared you might have found the house from the story. Then, when you disappeared, that's when I called them," pointing to our guests in our kitchen, who are surprisingly waiting patiently, "and told them everything you said before you left." She trails off.

Silence coats the room. I am full of jumbled emotions, ranging from furious that she never told me to finally happy that she did to confusion about what is to come.

"Okay, I have many questions and no idea where to begin," I say flatly.

"Please, ask the questions you have. Either myself or Shawn or Chloe will answer them."

Shawn and Chloe turn their heads and nod, letting Mom continue. "Please ask anything. It is about time I tell you everything. Again, I'm truly sorry for keeping it from you for so long."

I take a deep breath and figure out how or where to start.

"Okay," I say. "When I was younger and I disappeared, do you think I went to this place called Willorian?"

"Yes, it's the only place I can think of where you would have traveled to." She says with a hint of sadness in her voice.

"Okay, now do you think this stone I brought back could be a dragon scale, like the one from the story?"

She shutters, "I do believe so," as her words trail off.

Do I show her the stone, which now I conclude is a dragon scale, or do I wait?

Deciding to wait, I slide the stone into my backpack and continue my questions.

"You did research at the hospital but didn't find anything. Why is Dad always leaving?"

"I..." she started, but I interrupted her before she could say another word.

"I heard you guys the last time he was home. He has to leave to figure out what is going on, to find out *what* I am, and something about finding answers. Those were Dad's exact words."

Mom goes pale.

"You...You heard all that?" she stammers.

"Yes, now please tell me what it means."

With another deep sigh, she nods and begins once more.

"Your Dad has been searching for "portals" that connect this world, Earth, and Willorian. Ever since you disappeared as a baby, he has been fascinated by the concept of time travel and journeying between worlds. He works for a company that conceals its true research. By day, he drives trucks for other companies, but at night, they venture out searching for "breaks" in the universe and alternate event timelines.

They haven't had any luck for the last three years—until the day you told me about the house. That night, he called me and admitted they found signs of two breaks through the barriers, but the breaks vanished in an instant. Since then, they've been running tests where those breaks occurred, trying to recreate them, but no luck."

I sit there, speechless and in shock. *Dad works for a company that is trying to find where our world connects with Willorian.*

I feel like my whole life has been a lie, and now Mom has decided to throw it all in my face. My head is spinning, trying to keep it all straight. Dad hasn't come home he's more focused on figuring out these 'breaks' in the universe than on watching his son grow up. I am not okay with that. They're chasing something that could be futile. Do I fully believe everything she's telling me? I have yet to decide.

"Aidan, Aidan?" I hear my Mom's voice trying to break through the fog I'm in. I feel myself slowly turning to face her, but everything is still foggy. My mind struggles to make sense of the bombardment of information.

"Aidan, where did you get that?"

"What?" I say groggily.

"By your shoe, where did you get that?"

Looking down, I see what she's referring to.—the stone that appeared in my hand after the vision. It must have fallen out of my pocket, or perhaps I never manage to get it fully inside like I thought. I reach down, pick it up, and hold it in my hand, staring at it.

"Oh, I found a stone." Speaking to the rock more than my Mom.

"Aidan! You tell me right now where you *really* got that scale!"

"Scale? No, truly, it's a flat skipping rock, I think. Oh..." realization dawns on me. "I was standing outside after seeing their car logo, and it appeared in my hand after a vision. When I came back to reality, it was resting in my palm. I have no idea where it came from or why I have it."

Out of nowhere, Shawn and Chloe, the two people in our kitchen, look up as though waking from a trance and hastily walk over with open hands, trying to grab the stone or scale.

I quickly pull my arm back while keeping it away from their prying fingers.

"No, stop! I may not know where it came from or why I have it, but you cannot take it from me."

With that, I raced back out our apartment door and down the stairs to the large door that led outside once again.

10

Landing?

I run, sprinting as if my life depends on it. The air stings my face as countless tears stream down my cheeks. I hate that I'm crying, and I'm not even sure why. Maybe it's because Mom has lied to me my entire life, or because Dad has only been home a handful of times over the years. Whatever the reason, going back home is not an option—not until the Riverstone people leave. I don't want to talk to anyone. I just want to run away, for real this time.

Running past all the shops in town, I head toward the park. I don't slow down until my lungs are burning and begging for relief. Even then, my feet pound against the pavement with each determined step.

Finally, with my lungs screaming at me and on fire, my pace falters. Reaching out, my hand brushes against a tree as my body collapses against its trunk, giving in before my mind fully registers what's happening.

Time passes. Unaware of how much time has passed, I open my eyes and look around. The sky is clear, with white fluffy clouds forming shapes. Looking down, I examine the scale in my hand. My fingers are still tightly gripping its edges. I bring it closer to my face, examining it. Its shape is more oval with faint lines running down the center. As the sunlight strikes it, the scale shimmers, casting tiny glints of light."

Looking at it more closely, there's a hint of a reflection from above me. I'm caught off guard when a sound calls out.

"WATCH OUT!"

Too late for me to move, my eyes shoot up in time to see a light-skinned girl with long, dirty brown hair and big, round blue eyes fall on top of me. "OW!" I shout.

"Sorry, my bad. I'm still working on my aiming, especially with my landings." Echo chimes.

"Your landings?"

There aren't any branches above me. I'm leaning against a sapling, but she fell from the sky—straight down! Realizing she's still lying on top of me, I try to crawl out from underneath her.

"Hey, can you please move your leg off my back?" I ask her.

"Oh, sorry," she says sympathetically.

Once we untangle, I ask again. "Landing? Where are you coming from?"

"Willorian!"

11

Astral Projection is a Thing?

"You came from *Willorian*? How?" The questions spill from my mouth.

"Yes, of course! Where else would I have come from?" She exclaims.

"How? Wait a second. Do you fly, or is it considered time travel?" I ask, confused.

"Yes, of course she can! Technically, though, it's not flying," a new voice chimes in. "Echo can project through anything. It's called astral projection. Right now, she can move from one location to another, but she's still in the early stages of mastering her power. *She has been working on it for some time now,*" the new voice—a boy—mumbles quietly. "Echo is focusing on projecting herself over longer distances," the male voice said.

"Aidan, this is Calix," Echo says, rolling her eyes. "He's the first person I've been able to transport with me. I can astral project, but only briefly before I'm pulled back to Willorion. By the time my powers are fully developed, I'll be able to not only astral project but teleport!"

"Okay..." I say hesitantly. *Astral projection is a thing? Teleportation? At this point, I should accept that everything I hear about magic and powers is true.*

"So, we have to make this quick before we're pulled back to Willorian," Echo tells me. "Aidan, we need you to come back to Willorion. You could say there's been a...a turn of events, that we require your help."

"Oh, yeah, since you came to Willorian last time, things have changed—and for the worst. It's as if your arrival triggered a reaction, and things are rapidly changing," Calix says. "Echo told me she found you in the *Wishing Trees Forest.* How you got there is beyond our comprehension, but we need you to come back now and fix this," he pauses, waiting for me to say anything. "So..." he trails off, "now that we have delivered the message, you can come back, right?" he adds.

"I... I don't know," I start.

"What do you mean you don't know?" Calix asks, flustered.

"I don't know how to get back, nor do I know how I got there in the first place," I say sheepishly.

"What do you mean?" Echo asks, confusion creasing her brow.

"I don't know how I got to Willorion, and I don't know how to get back. It would be awesome to return," I say.

"Crap!" Echo shouts, starting to pace. "If you don't know how you got there in the first place, then it's gonna be nearly impossible for you to get back," Echo says, gesturing frantically with her hands in front of her face.

"Oh! I know! Tell us exactly how you got there last time. Maybe we can figure it out—don't leave out a single detail. I want to be bored by how many details you share," Calix says, shifting from side to side.

I pause, debating on what I should tell them. Technically, I've just met them, and I want to share everything that has happened to me in the last few days and even years. I'm not sure I want to divulge every single detail. But the truth is, I have no clue how I got to Willorian.

"Aidan!" I hear my name being called repeatedly. Shaking my head, I look back at them. Their bright and concerned eyes stare back at me. Shaking their expressions off, I stand up and start pacing back and forth, deciding to tell them what I experienced that day.

Taking a deep breath, I explain how I woke up late, the clock showing the wrong time, and then stepped—no, corrected myself—tumbled through the door to Willorian. After walking through the woods, I started to feel hungry and *wished* for food. Suddenly, apples and grapes began growing on the same tree. That's when Echo appeared and stopped me from eating them. *She was trying to warn me, but I didn't recognize her warning calls.* We continued through the woods, and right before exiting the woods, I was pulled out and somehow landed back home as though nothing happened. The clock was still showing the wrong time, and the door of my apartment building had closed.

I didn't tell them about the Riverstone people or the vision I had by the car—maybe I'll save those details to work through later.

"So you have no clue where you were?" Echo asks after I finish my story.

"That's what I've been telling you," I say.

"Wow, no wonder you were so dumbfounded when I was telling you about the forest. You had NO clue how to act there. I'll have to tell Dean to fire your instructor, but never mind."

"Who's Dean?" I ask, confused.

"Oh, he's an instructor where we grew up, but no need to worry about that," Calix chimes in.

Suddenly, both Echo and Calix's bodies start to flicker.

"Crap!" Echo says as their bodies keep drifting in and out of focus. "I thought we'd have more time. Okay, Aidan, before we disappear, please try to find another way to get back to Willorion. We desperately need your help. If I can, I'll try my best to come back." With that, they disappear entirely.

—

After the sun disappears behind the horizon, I head back home, praying the Riverstone people have left. Relief fills me when I arrive at the front of my building, noticing the Riverstone's car is no longer parked in front of my apartment building. Remembering the older lady with the cell phone and large hat, I look around hesitantly, seeing that the coast is clear. With my mind clearing, I head up the steps and push the big, heavy doors.

Entering the building, I see an empty trash can near the mailboxes, and the clock on the wall reads 7:23. Everything is back to normal, as though nothing happened.

As I reach the door to my apartment, I take a deep breath, clearing my mind of today's events, and push open the door. I look around, but Mom is nowhere to be found. I notice she's left dinner on the stove, but after today's events, I'm not hungry.

Pushing open my bedroom door, I see my bed is still in disarray. Glancing over, I notice a new book lying on the comforter. Walking over, I pick it up. It's leather-bound, homemade, and old. The pages stick out unevenly and are not properly aligned when it's bounded. Sitting on the corner of my bed, I open the cover and make out the rough scribbles written inside.

```
Findings of David,
Finding the Mythical Creatures and Rips in the World.
For my son, Aidan.
```

12

Dad's Journal.

```
"Findings of David,
Finding the Mythical Creatures and Rips in the World.
For my son, Aidan."
```

"Dad? Dad wrote a book for me." I say out loud, not intending to.

"David—your dad—made a copy of what he'd discovered from work for you the last time he was here," Mom says, leaning against the door frame. "He created it so that, if and when you learned everything, you could refer to what he had already found. Maybe it could help you."

I stare at Mom blankly, my mind racing. I want to flip through all of the pages and learn everything.

After a few quiet moments, Mom asks, "Would you like me to stay or leave?" I can see hurt in her teal, blue eyes, from our earlier conversation, but I don't know if I want to discuss it now.

"Would you mind if I flipped through the pages now, and we could talk about it later?" I ask softly.

"Yeah, that's alright. Take your time," she says, nodding repeatedly. She slowly turns away, and I wait until I hear her bedroom door shut to flip to the next page. I feel terrible, but I need time to process everything that has happened in the last few days.

Flipping through the book's pages, I first notice a handwritten index page. It lists the names of the U.S. states—some crossed out with a single line, others with multiple lines, and a few so heavily scratched out that the pen has created holes in the middle of the names. The following pages are filled with various symbols and shorthand, making them difficult to understand. Instead of attempting to decipher each word or symbol now, I continue flipping through the pages. After a few more turns, I jump when I see a page with *Origin HOUSE* scrawled at the top.

Skimming the page, I search for any clue about the house. My eyes scan the text:

"Origin house: a house housing all magic.
It is the "power source" for everyone and everything in Willorian. Whoever finds and gains access to the house can and will become the most powerful Unnatural ever. However, they must undergo extensive training to harness this power. Though it is possible, no one should attempt it.
No one should be able to find the house, but the house can choose to show up anywhere at any time.
No one knows what will happen if the house is found and if it allows an Unnatural to enter its premises."

Most of the information is somewhat familiar, but it's enlightening to learn more. There's a sketch of the house on the page, but it doesn't resemble the mystery house, the house I've seen. Hastily, I turn a few more pages and only to pause when something else catches my attention. I carefully riffle back to the page, trying not to tear or smudge anything.

"Rip(s) in between Earth and Willorian:
A Rip is similar to a portal, appearing between Earth and Willorian for only a few short minutes or even seconds. The only way to get back is to find another Rip. Only a handful of Rips have been created/sighted in the last twelve years. When searching for previous present Rips, look for dead grass or plants at unusual times. Sometimes, strange, unexplained weather doesn't align with standard patterns. I found a deceased two-headed bird surrounded by a mile-long stretch of dead grass at one location. After some calculations, I realized this Rip occurred the same time Aidan vanished on my watch while Sara was at work.
During my exploration, I encountered two other scientists searching for similar phenomena: unexplained crop circles, dead animals and plants. Their beliefs centered around aliens. Maybe that's what the Unnaturals are, but I want to believe that magic exists. Perhaps that's where Aidan belongs or where he comes from. The two scientists told me they found a "power source," and when they started getting close to it, one of them collapsed due to an odorless,invisible gas emitted from the Rip. They didn't have much more information, but I experienced a heavy, nauseating feeling near one of the larger

Rips I have found. Unfortunately, I never saw one while it was still active, but one day I will. The scientist shared some secrets on how to find their "alien" evidence:

Look around for a vast space of dead things, even a potted plant in the middle of summer, if the plants have been watered and cared for.

There will be no animals within a half-mile radius. If any are present, they've died in strange ways.

Once a Rip is discovered, it may feel like a force field is blocking the way, as though it is "locked., -- there is no, way to enter or harness it.

Be prepared! It's unknown what one might find or how long you could be lost if you find an active Rip. Bring food, water, a flashlight, -andeven if it sounds -ridiculoustell someone where you're going. Learn calling signals or Morse code. There's always a way to communicate. Bring backup defense tools:--whether a knife, sword, gun, or chemicals,--bring something to defend yourself.

Aidan,

If you are reading this, I hope you're safe. I wanted to watch you grow up, but I also needed to find out what these things are, and I hope it helps you grow. Your mother and I didn't know who or what you were when your mother found you, but we fell in love with everything that makes you...YOU. The day you disappeared for hours and reappeared, you were holding a glistening stone. It was pure magic. I had always believed as a kid, and even as I grew up, I secretly continued to believe. Other adults would look at me strangely for still believing in "magic," but a large part of me wants to prove it exists. Truth is, I may have gotten too caught up in it and forgotten to come home a few times, but I never stopped loving you. I love you and your mother, and I will be home soon, son.

Love Dad."

The last passage was dated well over three years ago. Thinking back, that was the last time Dad was home. I didn't realize I was crying until a tear ran down my cheek, almost landing on the journal. I brush it away before it touches the paper. Dad is proving that magic exists while he's "working." He discovered that Rips occur when magic happens on Earth. I wonder if another Rip appeared when the house did.

Looking up from Dad's notebook, I realize my room has significantly darkened. It's surprising that I was able to read his faint handwriting without struggle.

Flipping back a few pages to the last passage, something else catches me off guard. Dad's rules of going through a Rip are similar to Echo's rules for navigating the Wishing Trees, though with some key differences. The emphasis on carrying extra weapons for self-defense—rather than relying solely on powers or magic—and the importance of knowing various calls or signals stand out. It seems these rules are specifically for humans, those without magic, much like the Unnaturals.

Realization hits me like a bolt of lightning: I might have a way of getting to Willorian and seeing Echo and Calix again! If I follow the signs to find a Rip, there's a chance. Dad said they're rare, but with everything that has been happening, maybe—just maybe—I can find one.

Looking at my clock, I see it now reads 9:45. I'll need to check out the house's location tomorrow to see if there are any signs Dad mentioned. I also need to figure out if, by some chance, the house is connected to the Rips.

13

All Day Pass!

Sleep evades me. My brain is wired, and I can't keep my eyes closed. I begin counting the stars on my ceiling. *When I was younger, I always wanted the glow-in-the-dark stars that you could arrange however you wanted on the ceiling. My mom ended up getting them for my birthday.* There are ten small stars and eleven large ones. Even though they've been on my ceiling since I was five, I continue to recount them repeatedly, hoping it will make my eyes heavy.

After an hour of counting, I realize I'm not getting any sleep tonight. Throwing my legs over the side of the bed, I head over to my desk. My school stuff is spread out, having never made it into my backpack a few days ago. I push it all to the side to clear some room. When a textbook teeters over the edge, cringing, I shut my eyes tightly, bracing for the crashing sound of the textbook hitting the ground, but nothing happens. Slowly opening my eyes, I see the textbook still on the edge of the desk. I wrap my fingers around its edges and gently lay it on the floor. I don't want to worry about waking mom on her night off.

I grab some blank paper and sketch pencils and start to draw. I sketch everything: first the house, then Echo and Calix. I can't capture Calix in great detail since I've just met him, but I manage to get a general idea of his appearance. After finishing his drawing, I start drawing the dragon scales and all my "visions." I include as much detail as I can, determined not to forget a single thing.

—

When the sun shines through the curtains the following day, I realize I must have fallen asleep on my desk, still gripping my pencil. Looking down at my work, I see I started a new drawing. I review the ones I drew when awake, and then the new drawing sits with a tree in the front— it's of the Wishing Tree Forest, but there's something different about it.

In this drawing, the tree branches are laden with the food I was craving that day in the forest: apples, grapes, oranges, and even pizza, all dangling from branches. At the same time, the other trees in the drawing appear lifeless, as if their life had been drained out of them. Surrounding the trees are a few shadows shaped like people. The way I drew them, they resemble shadows more than actual humans. I can't tell if these represent real people or the spirits of those trapped in the trees. The trees have bare branches, devoid of leaves or pollen. Echo had mentioned that no one could tell which trees were the Wishing Trees, the sleep potion trees, or those that capture people—until it was too late.

—

Later that day, school returns to its "normal" routine, or as normal as it can be for me. I attend class, doodle when I'm supposed to be paying attention, and only get called on once. I struggle to answer, and the kids chuckle while trying to stifle their laughter. Surprisingly, I don't get sent to the office, and by lunchtime, I'm mentally checked out. I find my hiding spot and sit down with my lunch sack, pulling out my sketchbook.

Drawing has always been my escape. When I draw, I feel like I am being transported into my creations, leaving the chaos of my reality behind.

I don't even hear the bell until I feel a tapping against my shoe. Looking up, I see it's Janice, the receptionist. Based on her expression, it seems like she's been tapping against my shoe for a while.

"Hey, Aidan!" she says in a thrilling tone. "It's time for class, silly."

"What?" I ask, roughly as though I just woke up.

"It's time to go back to class."

"Ugh, can't you write me an excuse pass for the rest of the day?"

"I wish I could, especially since you're my favorite student."

"But you're not a teacher," I jokingly respond.

"True, but you are still my favorite student here."

I smile up at her in appreciation.

"Hey?" she says, changing the subject. "I haven't seen you in a few days. Everything okay?"

Do I tell her? Will she believe me? She's always been understanding of my struggles at school. Deciding against it, I once again keep everything a secret.

"Oh, I just wasn't feeling well," I lie, avoiding eye contact.

"Oh...that's too bad," she replies. "I hope you're feeling better?"

"I am, thank you," I say, smiling. Can you write me a pass to get out of school today?" I ask again, hopeful.

"You know I can't do that, but... I can write you a late-to-class pass."

—

After school, for old times' sake, I decide to head to the former Mystery House site. After reading Dad's journal and my brief visit to Willorian, I want to reminisce about the Mystery House I saw a few years ago. Walking up on the sidewalk, I'm speechless when I see it—the house. The Mystery House is back!

This is becoming a pattern: it appears, then vanishes, and now, it's here again. I haven't seen it in over three years. Why now? Looking at the house, I can tell—no, *feel*— that something is different. Scanning the perimeter, I start to recall what changed last time. No new windows or doors exist, and the air around me feels heavier and thicker. Glancing around, trying to remember Dad's journal and his list of things to look for. Mark's shop usually has flowers throughout the summer, but since it's fall and early winter, most flowers have wilted. Scratching that off my mental list, I continue to survey the area.

A few apartments above the shops are decorated with pots and flowers. There's one with a flower pot strewn on the balcony, and as I approach closer, I see the flowers are dead, gray, and wilted, but what's strange is the puddle of water dripping underneath the pot and onto the ground below it. Gotcha! Could a Rip be nearby?

I touch the gate, still feeling cold, but then the gate swings open as if pushed by the wind. I stare at it for a moment, unsure what to do. Before the house disappeared three years ago, I had tried kicking and even begged the gate to open, visiting it daily until it vanished. Today, with a dead plant on a balcony, it swings open as though it were nothing. After a long hesitation,

I walk through the gate—something I have dreamt about since I first saw the house.

I look up as I walk along the path, three cement stepping stones. The house looms above me, its peak stretching a mile up into the sky, and its chimney hints that something could be brewing in its fireplace. I focus on the front of the house, stepping onto the front step. Suddenly, without warning, I am pushed—not pulled—through the house at lightning speed. I tense when I see the house door isn't open, and I'm about to crash right through it. Bracing for impact, I close my eyes tight, waiting for the collision. But after a minute with no impact, I cautiously open my eyes, only to see my body gliding through it. The space around me blurs, and within a moment, I realize it: I am returning to Willorian.

Illustration drawn by Grace Bergeron

14

Something Glowing!

I think... I think I'm back in Willorian. Right? Where else could I be? But then again, I'm not entirely sure. I see a dense forest, thick with trees and moss as I look around. It's different from the Wishing Tree's Forest—I don't have the same sense of familiarity or comfort here. These woods are darker, colder, and a shiver runs down my spine, goosebumps prickling my skin. I struggle to lift my feet, only to glance down and realize I'm stuck in swampy water. With each step, my feet slosh, and water begins to seep into my shoes, soaking my feet.

Accepting the fate of soaked feet, I push through the thick water. A few moments pass before my foot catches on a rock, throwing me off balance. Thankfully, before I can collapse in the water, I catch myself, my hands landing in the water before falling face-first and getting an extra bath today. I take a deep breath and fill my lungs with the forest air. I try to regain my footing as my hands search the water below, trying to get a sense of where I am. I feel around until I discover a moss-covered rock. It must have been the one my foot caught on.

Moving around the rock, I notice it's not massive, but it's hard to grasp it due to the slippery moss and water coating its sides. Instead of attempting to balance and climb it, I decide to pick it up and move it. Curling my fingers around its edges, I count to three and pull upward. But just before the rock breaks free, the ground beneath me shifts, and the water begins to stir.

The Earth rears up and throws me backward. I fly out of the water, landing on a grassy patch. I'm thankful for my backpack, which cushions my fall—*I guess textbooks do have a practical use.* Looking up, I see the moss-covered rock now resting atop a massive, giant rock, perched at least thirty feet above me and on the back of a troll. *I was standing on the back of a troll!*

The troll is massive! Its shoulders brush the leaves of the surrounding trees. Its rock-like body is gray and caked in mud, with smaller rocks clinging to its rock skin. What I didn't anticipate was the smell. The stench had been contained when it was submerged underwater, but now, standing above the surface, the horrendous odor is unleashed. It's worse than forgetting to take the trash out for a few weeks before leaving for vacation. It's as if every food item has rotted beyond recognition, and nothing could mask the smell.

I try to cover my nose and mouth, realizing my hands are covered in swamp water and mud. The odor starts to burn my nostrils and make my eyes water. Now fully standing, the troll swings its thick arms, as if searching for me, perhaps thinking I'm the same height as it. I catch a fleeting glimpse of something flashing between its boulder-sized legs—just a brief figure—just a fleeting glimpse of a figure—before a few leaves fall to the ground.

Shifting my attention from the troll, I spot a massive tree trunk about three feet to my left. *If I crawl on all fours like a crab, I should be able to get behind it before the troll notices.* As soon as I take my first crawl step, I curl in place as the troll hurls a boulder against the tree I was hoping to take shelter. The boulder shreds the tree into toothpicks. I freeze, unsure what to do next. The troll's aim must be poor, but I'm grateful for that right now. Maybe he was trying to scare me—mission accomplished.

Movement catches my eye near his rock leg again, and I see it more clearly this time. It's a figure wearing a hooded cloak, its features remaining indistinguishable. One moment it's there, then it's gone. I blinking, trying to clear my vision, checking to see if the figure disappeared, when the troll roars, "Woke me, must die!" Another boulder flies straight toward me.

I should move, I need to move, I really need to move, but I can't. I feel paralyzed in place. Just before it crashes into me, the mysterious figure appears before me, raising his hands above his head and chanting. The boulder freezes mid-air and disintegrates into dust.

My eyes widen in shock, and I realize I've been holding my breath. It takes me an extra long moment to regain my senses, allowing my brain to catch up with what's happening. A raspy male voice coming from above snaps me back into reality.

"MOVE!"

I snap out of my stupor, gasping for air as I scramble to my feet. My backpack slaps against my back with each hurried step. I dash toward another tree to the right and hide behind its trunk. Bending over, I place my hands on my knees. I focus on my breathing, my heart racing in my chest.

Peering around the tree trunk, I see the hooded figure moving closer, standing between me and the troll. The figure is still holding his hands up, destroying every boulder that comes his way. The troll has ceased his anger.

The hooded figure approaches, grunting as he struggles to carry something heavy. As he turns, I see it: a glistening sword, polished steel, and with an edge so sharp it looks unreal. The hooded figure moves his sword toward me, the tip close to my face. Gulping and fear-stricken, I back up against the tree. Imagining the damage it could do. *Is the cloaked figure going to impale me? Why would he save me from the troll only to stab me? I wish I could vanish, sink into the tree, and hide from both threats—the figure and the angry troll.*

As I try to make myself disappear into the tree with no luck, I hear a branch snap in front of me. I close my eyes tightly, praying for a quick death. When another branch snaps nearby, I slowly open my eyes to see the cloaked figure shaking the sword in my direction. *Is he trying to give it to me? It would be helpful if he would speak and tell me what he wants.* I take a hesitant step toward the figure, reaching my shaking hand out to him.

"Take!" he grunts in a raspy voice.

Reaching out my trembling hand, I grab hold of the sword's hilt. The cool metal feels surprisingly lightweight against my skin. It's about two to three pounds and roughly thirty inches long. The hilt has a circular end, but there's something different about the metal. It doesn't quite match the metal on the rest of the sword. Before I can fully admire the weapon, the figure starts gesturing with his sword.

The sword, which I'm unsure where he was hiding given its considerable size compared to the one he gave me, is now in his hands. He gestures between his and mine, demonstrating how to hold it. I attempt to mimic his movements, trying to match his hand placements. At first, I grip the sword with both hands along the hilt, but he grunts and shakes his hand, signaling I should hold it with one hand. Following his instructions, I adjust my grip and watch as he demonstrates how to hold and swing it above his head.

I just received impromptu sword-handling lessons. Hopefully, these instructions will keep me alive long enough to get out of here.

Nodding in what I assume is approval, the figure lifts his cloaked head. That's when I hear them before I see them—bright green dots are falling from the sky, emitting piercing screams.

I hear them more than I see them. Their squawking is loud and shrill, like human screams at a higher pitch. As they get closer, I make out their pure black bodies and piercing green eyes that hurt to look at. I'm torn between covering my eyes or ears.

I duck my head and glance over at the cloaked figure. Not only is he not covering his eyes or ears, but he's fighting the birds with his long sword. He swings with great strength and precision.

"Sword. Birds!" he shouts over heavy breaths and sweeping sword swings.

Lifting my arm, I hold the sword, feeling its weight. Despite being roughly two to three pounds, it's a weight I'm not accustomed to. Taking a swing in the air, I aim for nothing, only getting a feeling of the sword. It feels good, like an extension of my arm.

I raise my sword and swing at an incoming black bird with green eyes. As I slice it in half, I expect to see a limp, lifeless bird body on the ground, but instead, the bird turns to ash and dust before it even hits the ground. They disintegrate like the boulders did with the figure's magic.

I take another swing and cut three birds this time, all turning to dust littering the ground. Looking up toward the sky, I see more birds emerging with no end in sight. I glance at the cloaked man and see at least ten birds swarming around him. He has dropped his sword and is now raising his hands, chanting. The birds all fall to the ground, but they don't turn to dust this time.

Turning back toward the sky, I see the endless stream of birds flying toward me. I begin swinging my sword repeatedly as I move in a circle, slicing anything that comes into contact with my blade. One bird flies straight toward me, missing the blade and instead slicing my upper forearm with its razor-like beak. It cuts through my sweatshirt and shirt, drawing blood that starts running down my arm, carried by gravity.

After what feels like an hour, both of us are panting, and my arm feels like it's on fire. With one swing of his sword, the birds suddenly stop. They vanish as quickly as they appear. Amid the chaos, I almost forgot about the troll. I wonder if he returned to his resting spot in the water.

Looking up and around, I see no birds anywhere in the forest, nor do I hear any. It's as if they've completely vanished. Seizing the brief respite, I slide off my backpack and spill out its contents. A few textbooks, pencils, an empty water bottle, and forgotten gym clothes tumble out.

Assessing my arm, I see crimson blood seeping around the open wound and the fabric of my clothes. I grab a shirt from my gym clothes and rip it into shreds. Using what I learned in my Natural Wonders class, I wrap the fabric around my arm, using my teeth to hold it in place as I pull the other piece under it to secure it—creating a makeshift tourniquet. Wincing as I tighten it, I ensure it's firmly in place.

After shoving everything back into my backpack and securing it on my back, I grab the sword I had dropped and go to stand. That's when I hear a low growl in the distance. Slowly rising and turning my body, I face the sound of freezing when I see two glowing eyes about fifty feet away. The creature begins to move toward me, its pace gradually breaking into a loping run. I try to make out what it is as it gets closer, now only about thirty feet away.

The creature is a large wolf, its fur mangy and unkempt. It has two bright yellow eyes, but there's something even more unsettling: a bright blue eye in the center of its forehead. Its teeth are bared in a vicious snarl, saliva dripping from the corners of its mouth.

My feet feel numb, and I can only hope—no, pray—that it will pass me. But deep down, I know it's futile. The creature has seen me, and it wants me. I close my eyes, bracing for the inevitable Then, I feel a large body behind me.

Opening my eyes, I see the cloaked figure standing there, his cloak wrapping around us. In an instant, we vanish.

Illustration drawn by Grace Bergeron

15

Today's Events.

We appear outside of a clearing of trees. It reminds me of the clearing near the Wishing Trees, but now, beyond the horizon, I can see tall, old buildings. They look like rundown hotels or apartments, their façades crumbling and forgotten.

A movement to my left catches my attention. The cloaked figure is shaking off his cloak, as if dusting it off. While he does this, I look closer, trying to discern who—or perhaps what—he is. His face is concealed, coated in black, as though he's wearing a mask covering his eyes, nose, and mouth.

The cloak is tan, buttoned up tightly around his neck, and I'm honestly surprised it hasn't choked him with all the movement he's been doing. As I scan him further, I notice leather gloves covering his hands and sturdy, heavy work boots on his feet. As he finishes dusting off his cloak, I spot silvery dust formations on the ground around him. The cloaked figure looks up, nods at me, and then vanishes!

Disbelief washes over me. Here I am, standing on top of a hill, surrounded by trees, with no idea where I am, and he *vanishes—poof, gone! What?* I start pacing back and forth, kicking pebbles at my feet, trying to figure out what to do next. I have no idea where I am or how I'll get back home. I'm about to give up and sit on the ground until nighttime, hoping that maybe Willorian will kick me out and send me back home, when I hear laughter below the hill.

Deciding I have nothing better to do, I head down the grassy hill, hoping whoever is below can help me. Walking down the slope is more complex than expected. I have to lean backward to avoid losing my footing. I only slip a few times but manage to catch myself until I hit a rock and go flying. The ground beneath my feet is unforgiving as my feet slip out from underneath me. My breath catches in my throat as gravity pulls me down the slope. The ground beneath me is jagged with rocks and small sapling trees as they scrape my bare skin from its sharp edges. Each of my limbs are thrashing in the wind. My heart pounds in my ears as I continue to fall between the two sets of tree lines. An unexpected wild cry escapes my lips, but it only meets the rush of the wind as I continue my tumble. I can't tell when my tumble will end, but I hope it's soon.

As my stomach begins doing flips of its own, I lose hold of my sword and backpack. I feel the pull of the hill lessen when my body meets the base of the mountain with a sickening thud. I land on a soft patch of green grass and lie there, looking up at the sky, watching the clouds drift above me. Slowly, I move my fingers and toes to ensure I haven't broken anything when I hear the laughter again, closer than before. My eyes drift closed as I lay in the sun, letting the sounds come nearer. When the laughter is only a few feet away, I begin to recognize the voices. I open my now tired and soreeyes and lift my head in time to see Echo and Calix coming over the ridge.

"Aidan?" Echo exclaims. "Aidan, is that you? You look like crap."

Sitting up, I reach for my temple, where a raging headache is forming. I pull my hand in front of my face and, thankfully, see no blood.

"Oh, Aidan, you look terrible. What happened, man?" Calix echoes Echo's question.

I look at both of them and then down at my arm, where the shirt is still tied around it and stained crimson. Echo grimaces and Calix briefly looks away.

"Here, let's get you up," Calix suggests.

They both move behind me, grabbing my arm and elbow to lift me. Once I'm standing, my vision blurs at the edges, causing me to sway and collapse into Echo.

"Whoa! Okay, maybe we should have you sit for a while," Echo exclaims.

They gently lower me back down on the ground and sit beside me.

"Okay, now tell us what happened to you," Calix says.

I recount everything: being sucked back into Willorian, landing in the swamp, waking the troll, the mysterious cloaked figure saving me and handing me a sword to fight off evil birds, and then disappearing before a three-eyed wolf could eat me— ,finally, tumbling down the hill.

"I have a question," barks Calix. "You mentioned a sword. Did this mystery person take it back, or do you still have it?"

Remembering that I lost it during my tumble, I scramble to my feet, only for my vision to blur again. Sitting back down, I tell them, "I lost both the sword and my backpack about halfway down the hill." I point up toward the hill.

"Okay, you stay here, and I'll go find them for you," Calix offers.

"Are you sure?" I ask.

"Yes, you are in no shape to go back up that hill and come back safely. We need you alive—can't have you die on us yet."

That catches me off guard. "What?" I start, but shake my head, hoping he was only joking. "Thanks," I continue roughly.

Calix heads off, heading back up the hill I just tumbled down.

"While he's finding your sword and backpack, tell me about the creatures you encountered," Echo says.

I recount every creature I encountered while she nods continuously. Once I finish, she pauses, thinking for a moment, then speaks up.

"You've had quite the adventurous day, haven't you?" She chuckles. "Okay, let's recap. First, you land in a swamp, which must have been The Venom Marsh. There are two swamps in Willorian, but the other one is nearly impossible to access, even by magic. Plus, the heat alone can kill you if you get too close. It's near a volcano that has only ever erupted once in the last century, but it's expected to erupt again sometime in the next couple decades."

"The troll you encountered sounds like a Moss Bog. There are only three in existence. They live year-round in the swamps where they won't be bothered. They're basically big, lazy babies, but if you disturb their slumber, they'll fight to the death—and most likely, it will be your death. Oh, and their method of defense is their smell. It's the worst stench you've ever experienced."

"I learned that the hard way," I say with a chuckle.

Echo laughs. "Yeah, they usually hide if any trouble comes their way. Like I said, they're babies. Now, the birds are interesting. They sound like Carals. Based on your descriptions, they match them exactly, except they usually only come out at night. Their bright green eyes are sensitive to sunlight, which can physically hurt them, causing them to go blind and then mad. They prefer living in darkness, which explains the trees for shade, but they usually eat insects and small rodents on the forest floor. They can't swim, so it's odd they were in the swamp. How many did you say there were?"

"Honestly, I don't know the exact number. At one point, I had roughly thirty to forty surrounding me, and the cloaked figure was fighting the same amount."

"That's even more interesting. They usually only fly in groups of ten, and no more. To have that many suggestions is a distress call. It's unsettling. Now that I think about it, I wonder if it's connected to everything happening here."

"Everything going on? What's going on?" I ask eagerly.

"Never mind, we'll fill you in later. The birds originated about a hundred years ago. They're not evil, but they're not good either. Really, the only notable thing about them is their beaks. They're sharp enough to cut through nearly all material forms, as you've found out by the look of your arm. You're lucky they didn't cut through to the bone."

I can still feel my arm throbbing from the tourniquet pushing on my wound. I'm also grateful their beaks didn't cut down to my bone.

Echo leans forward and slightly loosens the tourniquet. The blood has finally clotted, and the blood on my shirt and sweatshirt has since hardened. *At this point, I'll probably have to toss both of these after all this is over.*

"Now, continuing, this wolf you told me about—are you sure it had three eyes?"

"Yes, two bright yellow ones and a bright blue one in the middle of its forehead."

"Hmm, it sounds like a version of Yarbras. Yarbras are mangy-looking wolves, but they usually have two white eyes with a gross-looking fluid oozing out of the creases..." She goes silent, then shakes her head as though trying to erase the thought.

"What?" I ask, sitting up straight.

"No, nothing. It can't be."

"Tell me. Please. Even if you think it's insignificant."

"Ugh, okay. There's a possibility it could be Aiyana. But she hasn't been seen or heard about in centuries—she's as old as Willorian."

I repeat the name over and over in my head. Aiyana. Aiyana. Aiyana.

"What is special about Aiyana?" I ask.

"I don't know much about her, but legend says she is a seer for the animals. They say she can predict the end of time. Or at least that's what they say. No one knows much about her."

"So, why would she show up in the middle of a swamp after a troll and green-eyed birds attempted to kill me."

"I don't want to jump to any conclusions right now. Let's put a pin in that thought for later."

We sit there silently for a few minutes when we hear whistling from the bottom of the hill. Calix is walking back with my backpack slung over his shoulder and swinging my sword as though it's a baton rather than pure steel.

"Hey, Aidan!" he shouts. "Did you know you have an arming sword?"

"A what?" I ask, confused.

"An arming sword, sometimes known as a knightly sword.

This thing is sick! It's so cool, and even the hilt is unique. The pommel—the circle at the end of the hilt—is unlike anything I've seen before. It's not made from the usual metal. I'm not sure exactly what it is, but the whole thing is so cool. Can I have it?"

I know he's joking, and I've only had it for a few hours, but his comment makes me feel oddly protective over it. It's a sword, and I'm protective over it? What is happening?

"Um, no," is all I can manage.

"Oh, darn," he says with a chuckle. "That's okay. I'll have to have one made because this are cool! Where did you get it?"

"The cloaked figure when we were fighting off the birds."

"Ah, man, that's cool. What birds were they?"

Realizing he had been gone and hadn't heard the whole story, Echo speaks up.

"Hey, how about we show you what's been going on in Willorian while we tell Calix more about your morning? Are you okay to stand?" she asks.

"I should be," I say with a smile. With that, they help me up again, and I pray I don't fall again.

16

My Drawings Are Real?

As we walk, Echo and I fill Calix in on everything.

"Wow, dude, you've had an interesting day. Hey, do you know how you're getting to Willorian from Brooklyn?"

I still don't feel comfortable sharing details about the house. If it's connected to the theories about the dragon scales and the magic of Willorian, I need to be cautious. Once one person knows, it's only a matter of time before everyone finds out.

"I was walking on the sidewalk one minute, and the next, I was in the swamp," I say instead. It's not an outright lie, just not the whole truth.

"Interesting," Echo and Calix say in unison.

We've been walking for some time, and it seems like we're not getting any closer to the buildings I saw earlier. I think we're headed east, but navigating directions was never my strong suit. I'm unsure of our location until I spot it: the entrance to The Wishing Tree Forest.

"What are we doing here?" I ask, glancing at Echo and Calix for answers.

"Remember when we visited and mentioned that things have been happening in Willorian?" Calix shudders.

"Yes?" I reply nervously.

"Well, we need to show you what those weird things are," Calix says.

We take a few steps forward, and somehow, we find ourselves in the middle of the forest as though those few steps transported us there. I feel nervous until I begin to look around.

"See, this is what we wanted to show you!" Echo says, extending her arms out in a sweeping gesture.

Looking around, I understand why they needed me to come back. All of the trees in The Wishing Trees Forest have random items hanging from them—everything from food of all kinds, candy, fruit, and hamburgers to toys and electronic gadgets. Even more surprisingly, a few trees are dangling money from their branches. Beyond The Wishing Trees are countless useless wishes; I see a hundred trees with ashen-colored bark. They have no leaves, and some even have human-sized holes in their trunks. Realization dawns on me—those must be the ones that "capture" people.

This all feels weirdly familiar, but I'm not sure why. I wonder if The Wishing Trees are actually the generous trees, and the trees capturing people are using the poison pollen from another tree. They must have used The Wishing Trees to lure others in.

Standing there, I'm struck with a sudden realization. I recognize this scene playing out before me! I frantically reach for my backpack, grabbing my sketchbook, and start flipping through the pages.

"What are you doing? We don't have time for you to look through your drawings or to draw right now!" Calix exclaims.

"No, no, I'm not going to draw, but I think I already have.

Exactly this!" I say, still flipping through the pages.

"What do you mean?" Echo asks, coming closer to me.

Finally, I find the right page and show it to them.

"The night I was sent back, I drew all night, capturing everything I saw. I have no memory of drawing this, but it's here. I must have kept drawing after I passed out. Somehow," I murmur softly.

"You drew this before?" Echo questions. "Hey, what's your power again?"

My power? I'm confused. I'm showing them a drawing I did. I knew I had access to Willorian, but I didn't think I could have a power directly connected to Willorian.

"Aidan!" she shouts

"What?" I ask, snapping out of my thoughts.

"Ugh, you really need to stop disappearing into your head," She chuckles, trying to stay serious.

"Oh, yeah. Sorry, it's a bad habit." I chuckle.

"That's okay. What I was asking was, can I see your sketchbook?"

"Sure..." I say hesitantly, feeling confused.

Handing her my sketchbook gives me mixed feelings. I fear the drawings won't live up to her expectations. *I haven't shown many people my artwork, and I'm anxious about their reactions. Reading and writing have never been my strengths, but drawing has always been my way of expressing my thoughts and feelings.*

She starts slowly turning the pages, beginning with drawings of various mythical creatures I've daydreamed about. I've considered adding them to my comic books once I start writing them. As she continues to flip through, she reaches the scenes from the house, and I silently pray she doesn't ask me about them. I blush when she flips to the page of her and Calix. I forgot I included them in this sketchbook.

"Is this me?" she asks, blushing.

Why is she the one blushing?

"Yeah… I wasn't sure if I'd see you, well, both of you, again, and I wanted to draw you guys. I find that when I draw things, I remember them better," I explain.

"Aw, that's sweet of you. Wow! You really captured my bright blue eyes. That's talent!" she says.

"Thanks," I reply, trying to hide my stupid grin.

"No, really, Aidan, these are genuinely good. They're practically lifelike."

A blush rests on her cheeks as she flips through a few more pages. She pauses on a particular drawing, staring at it for a long moment.

"Is this… no, this can't be," she says, her voice trembling slightly. "Calix, is this what I think it is?"

Echo and Calix exchange glances, their expressions a mix of shock and confusion. The gravity of the situation is settling in, and I can almost see the wheels turning in their heads.

"Holy crap! It is!" he exclaims.

"This war—what you've drawn— is not something anyone would know about, especially if they've never been to Willorian.

Confused, I watch as she turns my sketchbook around to show me what she's talking about. It's a drawing that spans two pages side by side and is shockingly detailed—far more so than anything I've ever drawn. It's the same drawing I created back in class three years ago. On one side, mythical creatures are fighting on a dusty path, while on the other side are warriors who appear human but have magical powers. Different colors of magic flow from their hands and even their eyes.

I'm shocked by the amount of detail in the drawing. It shows that the warriors have been fighting for a long time, each displaying signs of exhaustion and dark circles under their eyes. Suddenly, it hits me like a ton of bricks. That day in class, when I drew this, I sketched it in my textbook. I can still picture the textbook sprawled out before me, with the fight scene competing for space alongside the printed words. How did this drawing from my textbook end up on two sketchbook pages? Did I redraw it?

I look up from the sketchbook to see Echo and Calix staring at me.

"I drew this in my textbook three years ago. I dozed off during class, and when I woke up, I was in trouble, but this drawing—only smaller—was in my textbook." I explain casually, chuckling a little to lighten the mood. "Why? What's the significance of it?"

Echo looks skeptical.

"Aidan, I'm asking you, how did you know about this war? If you only recently came to Willorian and claim you know nothing about Willorian and the Unnaturals, then how do you know about this war and when it took place?" She speaks slowly, ensuring I understand her question.

"I don't know. I'm telling you the truth, and I have no idea!" I respond firmly. "Again, I was daydreaming in class one day, doodling in my textbook, when I was called on. It felt as though I was being pulled away from the war itself. I thought I was there. It was strange. I still remember it vividly. I could hear and see the dust swirling around the warriors. It was as if, with just a few steps, I would be able to smell the sweat coming off them. They looked like they had been fighting for a few days or weeks." I say bluntly.

Calix and Echo are now whispering to each other. I'm unsure when they started, as I was lost in thought of my explanation.

Calix breaks the silence. "I think I know what your power is, man!" His excitement is palpable.

"Okay..." I reply hesitantly, now feeling scared. *This could change everything for me. First, I was somehow transported to a new world, and then I learned that my parents had found me. It's as if I don't belong anywhere. Now, just when I thought I might have discovered a Rip in the world—a Rip my Dad has been searching for most of my life—I find out I have powers. My head is spinning. If they drop another bombshell, I might faint.*

"You're a Seeker, a rare and very powerful one at that! Not only do you have premonitions—clearly, since you saw, well, drew, what the forest would become after you left in such skillful detail—but you've also drawn both the future and the past. A past you know nothing about, not to mention only Unnaturals know about Willorian's history. We were taught it in school, but since you're from Earth, there's no way you would have known about it—especially three years ago. This war was the one that created the split between Unnatural people with powers, like us," he gestures, "and Unnatural beings, the mythical creatures. You've drawn them— though not all, but a handful. Had you seen any of these Creatures before you drew them?"

I shake my head, absorbing the information.

"Exactly! The Creatures not only have their own magical abilities, which are based on their families, but they also have the ability to adapt or gain more by winning battles against their opponents. If their opponents surrender, they absorb a portion of their power. The Unnaturals didn't agree with this, and it wasn't fair that the creatures were also born with strength, varying on the type of creature they are."

"The Unnaturals came together and agreed the Creatures shouldn't be able to gain more power by winning a fight. Some high-tech Unnaturals created a 'blocker,' which, as you might have guessed, would block any additional magic the victor would have gained from their opponent. Instead of magic being transferred to the winner, it would be dispersed back into the air of Willorian. For a while, this worked until some of the Creatures revolted. That's when the war broke out. Not only did no one win, but both sides lost a substantial amount of warriors. The war lasted five days and was finally stopped by a group of Elders on the fifth day. The Elders are the oldest citizens in Willorian, a mix of Creatures and Unnaturals. They reached an agreement: they would strip the Creatures of their magical powers, leaving them with only their original strength, while the Unnaturals would keep their powers— with one exception. If a Creature kills an Unnatural in a fair fight, the winner is awarded the former opponent's powers as a mark of victory. However, they couldn't go out seeking an Unnatural to fight. It had to be for a legitimate reason."

"With all the extra magic from the Creatures - since there are more Creatures than Unnaturals - the Elders couldn't release that much power into the air. They decided to store the excess magic in 20 dragon scales. Dragon scales are rare—almost nonexistent. They're not only fireproof, windproof, and waterproof but also indestructible. They chose 20 scales to contain the excess powers and then dispersed them throughout Willorian since they couldn't put them all in one location." He pauses to take a deep breath.

"Then there's the house. In the center of Willorian, there was a house—a safe haven for the super-rare Unnaturals and a repository of all knowledge about everything and everyone in Willorian. The super-rare Unnaturals included Creatures who had gained extra powers and other Unnaturals who were threatened because of their unique abilities. Both Unnaturals and Creatures could seek refuge in the house."

"There's a theory that the house has a lower level. If someone brings all of the dragon scales to the door of that level, it will reveal the heart of Willorian! Anyone who collects all the scales and gains access to the lowest room to uncover the heart of Willorian would have the power to take over the world, causing everything we know to burn."

"Burn?" I ask, suspicion evident.

"Yes," Echo cuts in. "Although possessing all the power in the world would be amazing, it would be too much for a single body to control. It would physically burn them—and everything around them."

Calix nods emphatically. "Which is why we need your help."

"How can I help? I haven't been in Willorian my whole life. I knew nothing about Willorian's existence till now. Please, tell me how I can help, because I'm confused," I shout.

Echo and Calix look at me in surprise.

"You clearly have a special gift, and I hate to admit it, but you might be the only one who *can* help save Willorian," Calix says with a heavy sigh.

Echo continues as if I hadn't interrupted their story. "There are indications that dragon scales have been discovered and are being used. The trees in the Wishing Forest have been stripped of their magic, causing the other trees to dry up and release their prisoners, and The Wishing Trees have exposed their wishes. That's why you see all the past wishes dangling from their branches. If a spark ignites in these woods, it would destroy the trees in an instant, and everything would burn… literally."

I wonder if my wishes are dangling off those trees.

After a long, awkward silence, I ask, "Does Willorian have firefighters?" I feel foolish for asking, but I need to break the uncomfortable pause between us.

"We do, though they're not like the firefighters on Earth," Echo responds.

"We have two different types of Unnaturals who handle our fires," Calix begins. "The first are Ondines. They can douse smaller fires; for example, if someone loses control of a bonfire or there's a small accident, they can control it with water. The second are Chanticos. Their powers come from volcanoes and hearth fires. They can absorb the fire, though they can be more of a liability. They're what we call wild cards. They absorb fires and live near the Lifeless Marsh, where nothing survives. However, if anyone makes them angry, they might release all the fires they've absorbed, bringing us back to square one. We only call out the Chanticos when we are desperate. Thankfully, most of Willorian's Unnaturals know the consequences of calling a Chantico, so we avoid causing a bigger mess."

"In my lifetime, I think I've only seen the Chantico's two or three times," Echo adds.

That must be amazing—having powers to absorb fire or control water. How cool!

"Hey, Calix, what's your power? I realized I don't know what it is." I say, trying to change the topic.

"Oh, it's nothing of importance. It's actually pretty mundane. Forget about it," Calix says, sitting back down on the ground and picking at the blades of grass. He pauses for a long moment, then adds, "We should start moving. It'll be dark soon." *His tone is somber. I wonder why he doesn't want to share what his power is. Echo must know what it is, given their friendship, but it's odd that it's a secret.*

Calix jumps up, brushing grass trimmings off his legs, and starts heading down the hill. Echo and I exchange glances. She shrugs, and we both follow in his footsteps.

"Is it just me, or is it quicker to walk out than last time?" I ask Echo in a whisper.

"It's due to the magic of the forest. With the magic waning, we should be able navigate through it faster than usual. When the forest is at its magic peak, it can trick its prey by drawing them toward the heart of the woods, trapping them. But since you were dropped in the middle last time, you didn't experience that pull. One notable thing about the forest losing its magic is that we don't have to worry about the rules and the risk of entrapment."

I consider this. The trees do possess magic, and whatever is causing them to lose that magic and their ability to trap people to death—or a near-death experience.

"This is a good thing, right? With the trees losing their magic, no one will go missing anymore, right?" I ask.

"That's true, but remember when we told you about the other creatures? The only way for them to gain magic or other powers from Unnaturals was to win in a fair fight," Echo says.

"Yeah?"

"Since the trees are rooted in place, the Elders figured leaving some of their magic would be okay. That's why half of the trees had magic, and the others didn't, and since the trees couldn't fight with any force or strength, the Elders thought it would be fine—or so they thought at the time. Since the trees revolted and worked together to *fight* the Unnaturals to gain their powers. That's one reason it's nearly impossible to distinguish between the poison pollen trees, the ones whose powers were taken away, The Wishing Trees, and the trees that absorb the body of an Unnatural. Sadly, this is the way this world exists. Even though The Wishing Trees were being used for evil, they are helping the entrapment trees to take power, which goes back to Willorian—more or less."

"I guess that makes sense," I say, reflecting on everything. *How can trees revolt?* I wonder to myself.

We're silent for an hour as we walk. My feet start to hurt, when I see the opening of the forest. As we cross the threshold, it feels as though the forest is releasing a sigh of relief.

I followed Echo and Calix down the hill and through the wooded areas. *I really like Calix and Echo; they bring out my curiosity, and I'd love to spend all my time here in Willorian and never return home. I can see myself becoming friends with them. I feel more... free. I don't have to hide my nervousness, anxious feelings, or my reading issues. I'm not afraid of asking what might seem like stupid questions. I can ask anything freely, not only because I'm learning everything here but also because I know I won't get made fun of. So far, they haven't asked me to read anything out loud.*

"Hey, Calix, what's your favorite movie?" I ask, breaking the silence and trying to learn more about him.

"Transformers!" He shouts, "What about you?"

"The Goonies," I chuckle, "it was one of my dad's favorites."

We continue asking each other silly questions, with Echo chiming in every once in a while. Toward the end of our questions, we discovered the three of us have quite a bit in common, which settled my nerves, but my confidence grew a little too high when I ask, "So, why won't you tell me about your power, Calix?" I ask again.

"Drop it, Aidan!" He says sternly, his mood turning.

"Oh, it must be really embarrassing," I say.

"Aidan, maybe you should drop it," Echo chimes in.

"I'm serious," Calix says again.

"Can I guess?" I ask.

"No!" He shouts.

"Hmm..." I mumble, "Oh, I know, do you have a siren voice? Is that why you're upset by it? You have a girl's power?"

"NO! Seriously, drop it, Aidan."

"Oh, is it jumping? You haven't learned all your abilities, so you can only jump six feet."

"Seriously, if you don't stop, I'm gonna knock you out."

"Oh, let me take one more guess."

"No! Weren't you not told *no* as a kid and love using it against me now?" He's shouting now.

"I was told no a lot as a kid. This is just fun."

"Aidan, I'm not proud of my power. So, please stop."

"Hmm..." I think hard, wondering if I can get him to spill his power. He's so agitated that I want him to explode. Maybe that will release his tension. "How about... Oh, I know. Do you turn into a hulk when you're mad, but instead of the angry green guy, you turn into a purple monster, and when you slam your hands on the ground, butterflies and rainbows shoot out of your palms? That's it, right?" I smile brightly, starting to laugh too hard. I almost crumble to the ground. My sides start burning with my laughter. I hear Echo trying to stifle a snicker behind her palm, failing miserably, as she begins to bend over laughing.

Clearing my throat and standing up straight, my premonitions could not have predicted what would happen next.

Looking up at Calix, I see his fist flying through the air and connecting with my cheek. The pain is unbelievable. I feel my face heating, blood racing to a spot on my cheek. Echo stops her laughter. I see she's now holding her face in surprise and horror. Calix is fuming. *I'm surprised there isn't smoke coming out of his ears. I guess he was serious when he said he didn't want to discuss his power.*

The initial shock of what happened has passed, and now I'm fuming. No—I'm pissed. Seriously? He punched me. Without realizing it, I'm swinging a punch straight toward his face, straight and center...or what I think is center. I've never thrown a punch before. Balling up my first, I aim and hit roughly to the left of his nose, under his eye. He stumbles backward.

"Are you kidding me, Aidan?" He starts breathing heavily, taking deep breaths as his face goes from a just-been-punched red to a fuming, deep shade of crimson.

"Wait," I ask in shock. "You're mad at me? You're the one that threw the first punch." I can feel the spot where he hit me starting to swell and bruise. I bet if I were to touch it right now, it would be hot.

I see Calix begin to fume and clench his fist again. He's going to throw another punch at me. He steps forward. I watch his body language. He swings when he steps forward, and his fist connects with my stomach, right below my ribs. The air in my lungs is immediately expelled. I can't...I struggle to take in air. My lungs are screaming for breath. I start to feel faint, and my vision starts to blur when I see Calix coming at me again with a raised fist. I have a split second to duck before he hits me again, but I don't know where he will aim this time. He already hit my face and stomach. I can barely make out his outline when I move slightly to the left, his fist missing the center of my chest but hitting my bandaged-up arm from Coral's razor beak. It isn't until my body collides with the ground that I realize I've collapsed. The pain radiates from...everywhere. I can't figure out which part of my body hurts the most. Between my cheek, stomach, and arm, I still don't think I have fully taken a deep breath in minutes. *I'm pretty surprised I haven't passed out from the lack of oxygen yet.*

Looking up toward Calix, I see that he is cupping his nose, and a crimson color is coating his fingers. I didn't think I hit his nose, but maybe the impact of hitting below his eye caused his body to react this way. I'm not sure where Echo is until I hear a blood-curdling scream in front of me, and Calix charges at me. One minute, I fear I might die from the lack of air or from Calix ending my life. But when I open my eyes, Echo is crouching over me, and Calix is no longer in front of us. Lifting my head, I see we are in a meadow full of yellow and white flowers.

"Where... where are we?"

"I transported us out of there. It was going to end badly, and no one is allowed to die today," she says, looking around nervously.

"You transported us? I thought you could only astral project."

"Yeah, I can astral project, but remember when I told you time works differently in Willorian? I told you it was a few days ago, but it was a month on Earth. I've been practicing and can finally transport myself and one other person. I haven't had any luck being able to transport more than one person."

"Months?" *Has it been a month since I've been home? In my last conversation with Mom, I told her I needed time to process everything, and then I disappeared.* A gut-wrenching feeling sits in the pit of my stomach. *Oh no, I feel like I'm going to be sick. What does Mom think?*

"Aidan...Aidan...you with me?" Echo is repeating.

"What? Wait, are you telling me it's been a month since I've been home on Earth?" I ask, my heart racing, waiting for her clarification.

"Yeah, or at least close to a month. I don't exactly know how the timing works, but a few hours here can equal two or three days on Earth."

That would explain why three days had passed since I came home for the first time in the Wishing Trees. The sickening feeling sinks in my stomach again.

"I...I need to go home. My Mom must be worried sick." I say, scrambling to my feet.

"Home? You can't go home. Willorian needs your help! We need your help." She follows me onto her feet. "Aidan, I'm sure your Mom understands that your Dad wants to learn things and your abilities. I'm sure she knows you didn't run away and you found yourself where you belong. You're parents..."

I cut her off. "My Dad? What do *you* know about my Dad?"

She stumbles over her words. "Well...I..."

"Echo! What do you know about my *Dad*?" I say more emphatically.

Before she could respond, a siren in the distance went off. It's so loud I have to cover my ears, afraid it might puncture an eardrum. Glancing up at Echo, I see she is standing perfectly still, with her eyes closed, as though she's trying to listen. Realization dawns on me; the siren isn't a siren but a message.

It's a long minute before the siren noise stops, and Echo takes a deep breath, turning to look at me.

"Aidan, I will answer all your questions later, but we have to go for now."

17

Abandoned Building.

Echo transports us to...well, I'm not quite sure where she transports us to. Looking around, one can see that it resembles a homeless camp. There are tents everywhere and not in any organized order. A large abandoned building stands in the background. There are people all around us laughing and crying, some working out, and some showing off what appears to be swords cr daggers. I spin around, trying to take in everything, when Echo shouts my name, sounding very distant. I stop spinning to see that she is twenty feet in front of me. I can tell my reaction amuses her. Looking up, I see strings of lights dangling off the tree limbs above. This is *home* for these people.

Echo makes a *come here* motion with her hands as I catch up to her

"Where are we?" I ask, still in awe, feeling bad that I thought this was a homeless camp.

"We're home, but you won't see the full effects until dark. That's when the real *magic* begins," she says, smiling as though she is holding onto a secret.

Echo leads me to the abandoned building. "We will be staying here tonight. Tomorrow, there will be a meeting to address the concerns about Willorian."

"Was that what the siren noise was?" I ask before I realize the words are tumbling out of my mouth.

"Siren noise? Oh, I wonder," she ponders briefly, "I bet you're not adapted to the sounds of the Babonshee. She—the Babonshee—has a line of banshees in her family, but instead of alerting her when a death occurs, Babonshee alerts her to signs of danger. She's our emergency alert system," Echo tells me. "I wonder if the sound is more of a siren than a scream?"

Thinking back to when we were in the meadow, I was frantically thinking about my Mom and how it's been close to a month, Earth time since I've been home. Then, hearing the sound. The ear-piercing sound. Thinking hard about it for a few seconds, I still couldn't decipher if it was a scream or a siren.

"I...I think it was a siren. That's what it sounded like." I say, still trying to process the last hour.

"Interesting! I wonder if you have to be in Willorian for a longer period of time to understand her." She says, while I can see her mind working.

Echo shrugs her shoulders, turns around, and leads me to the building—the one I thought was abandoned—but can now see life within its walls. Leading me to the main front doors, she pauses at the double doors, holding her hand toward the window panes. A bright light shines through the window. Between the window's glass, the light starts to shine brightly around her palm.

"Don't worry. We'll set you up later. If you choose, you can come and go as you please."

I don't say anything, only nod my head. When a clicking sound chimes from the door, it opens automatically. Stepping through the threshold, I'm beyond amazed by what I see.

On the outside, it looks like an abandoned building, maybe a school, but on the inside, it's completely different. There must be magic involved; this place is huge! Rooms line the perimeter, reaching three stories high. In the center lies a large courtyard full of different fruit trees and flowers. The ceiling is completely glass. People mingle about, paying us no attention.

Echo leads me to one of the rooms on the second floor.

"You can stay here tonight. This is an open room for anyone coming and going who only has a few things. They get placed into one of these five rooms," gesturing down the hall.

Echo reaches into her pocket and pulls out an old-fashioned skeleton key, dropping it into my palm. "I'm going to go take care of a few things, but I will meet back up with you in a bit," Echo chimes in as I unlock the door, letting it swing open as I take in the barren room. It is filled with a bathroom, a shower, a sink, and a toilet to the left and is fully stocked with towels. The main room holds a desk with a small lamp, a twin bed, and some old movie posters I'm sure past visitors have left. Walking in, I drop my backpack to the floor, hearing a loud metal clanking sound. Confused, I grab my backpack, place it on the bed, and unzip it. My sword, the one the mystery figure gave me, jumps out of the bag as soon as the zipper releases it from its confinement. I have no recollection of putting it in there, but maybe Calix or Echo did. I honestly forgot about it after everything today. Placing the sword on the desk, I grab hold of my sketchbook and pencils.

Realizing I smell ripe, I head toward the shower to clean up.

My reflection catches my attention as I walk past the mirror. Taking a few steps back, I center myself in the mirror to take in my overall reflection. I'm an absolute mess!

My hair is greasy, going in every direction, and I'm sure there is dirt and swamp muck caked into every strand. I have a multicolor bruise forming on my cheek from where Calix punched me. Raising my hand to my face, I wince at the pain flaring under my fingers as they lightly brush the bruise. *Well, that's going to be painful for a few days.* Removing my shirt, I notice the fist-size circle forming on my abdomen where Calix punched me.

My brain transports me back to the moment he punched me and how hard it was to take in a single breath, restricting air from entering my lungs. Pausing, I shake my head, clearing it of the memory and the pain. My eyes scan over all my bruises before moving to my arm, noticing the strip of fabric is still wrapped around my cut. I will need to clean it. Eventually, I begin to unravel the piece of cloth and again wince in pain when I pull it away from the wound, feeling it has fused to my skin. The wound begins to bleed a bit as I break the seal formed between the fabric and the wound.

I'll have to ask Echo where the nearest pharmacy is tomorrow. For now, I'll use water and soap to clean it.

Getting fully undressed, I step in the shower under the stream of warm water. Letting the water pellets wash away the day's dirt, sweat, and blood down the drain. I triy my best not to scream out when the water hit my wound.

Once I finish my shower and towel off, I am surprised to find a pair of sweatpants and a sweatshirt waiting for me on the bed in my new room. Sliding into both pieces of clothing, I instantly feel more relaxed. Climbing under the sheets, warmth and comfort envelop me, pulling me to sleep. Promising myself I would draw before bed, I open my sketchbook, but once the pencil touches with the paper, I fall fast asleep.

18

Knocking!

I wake due to the sound of heavy banging against a thick wooden door. Struggling to open my eyes, I look around the room, briefly forgetting where I am. My heart starts racing as my breathing picks up, and my eyes scan the room. *Where...where am I?* Realization dawns on me as the last few days flood my memory. Taking a breath and calming down my rising terror, I slowly climb out of bed. My feet touch the cold floor. Shivers shoot through my body, leaving a tingling sensation in its wake. Moving my hand, it brushes against my face. I feel the dull heat and a new, very swollen cheek under my right eye. I'm thankful I can still open my eyes—another round of banging rings out against the solid wood door.

"Yeah!" I shout back, letting whoever is on the other side of the door know that I am, in fact, alive and awake.

Stretching, I notice my sketchbook sprawled out and open to a new page. A drawing has been sketched out with thin, fine lines. The image depicts a shadow figure, where I can't distinguish any distinctive features. The shadow figure holds up his hands, and on the next page, there appears to be a dragon scale split in half, and what looks to be magic is flowing from it, heading toward the shadowed figure. The drawing is roughly sketched out, but if someone were looking at it, they would get a general idea of what it portrays.

Another round of knocking pounds against the wood panels of the door as I close my sketchbook while still contemplating the new drawing. Shuffling over to the door, I feel the tightness in my ribs with each movement. Reaching the door, I turn the knob-opening it slightly. I see Echo standing on the other side, grinning widely.

Opening the door wider, she greets me. "Good morning, sleeping beauty! How'd you sleep?"

"Hi!" I say sheepishly. "Good. I was out. How long was I asleep?"

"You've been asleep for close to three days."

"Three days? Seriously?"

"You've had some eventful days, and it would make sense."

"Yeah, but to sleep for three days...Wow." I can't believe it myself. Three days of sleep is insane.

"So, now that you're fully rested, are you hungry?"

"Famished."

"Perfect, but first—here," she holds out a square box with a red cross on it.

Smiling, I grab the box, moving toward the bathroom counter. I open it to see its contents spill out on the bathroom counter. "I was going to ask you where to get some ointments and bandages the other night, but clearly, I didn't do much after showering and passing out," I say, chuckling.

"Yeah, I bet you were wiped out, but let me look at that." Before I can react, she grabs my chin, pulling my face toward her. Feeling her warm hand touch my chin sends an unexpected shiver down my spine.

"Oh, that doesn't look pretty at all. He definitely hit you with all his strength. How are your ribs?"

"About the same. I can breathe now, which is good," I chuckle. I know she's friends with Calix and wants to help me, but I don't understand why she took my side and saved me. *Maybe she wanted to save the kid who was supposed to help save Willorian.* Whatever that means.

After applying the ointment and a fresh bandage to my cut, I pull my shirt sleeve back down my arm.

"How were the clothes? I snuck them into your room when you went to shower." she says, changing the subject.

"They're really comfortable," I tell her, smiling.

"Good! Well, now that you've slept and put fresh bandages on your wounds, are you ready for food?"

"Yes!"

19

Memorpastries!

We make it to the first floor and into a large meeting room, which is currently being used as a breakfast hall. I could smell the food before I walked in.

Seeing the vast spread of food was unnerving. There's so much food! There's everything from pancakes, cereal, eggs, sausage, bacon, pastries, and fruit—every fruit one could possibly imagine. I gawked at the sight of it.

"Are…is all of this free?" I ask, stunned.

"Yes! Why would you think we'd have to pay for it?" She asks, confused.

"I've… I've never seen this much food before. Who prepares it all?"

"We have chefs on site who prepare all of our meals, and all the fruit is grown here in Willorian. They look like normal breakfast items but have a little twist to them, " she says with a wry smile.

"What do you mean?"

"Here, try this. It's an egg, but it's from a Willorian chicken."

Reluctantly taking the egg, I hold it in my hand. The egg is hard-boiled. I bring it up to my mouth nervously. I look over and see Echo nodding and smiling. *Honestly, I should have made her take the first bite. I assume it's not poisonous, but I have no idea what to expect.* I take a small, tentative bite and pull back in surprise. It's sweet but delicious. The egg yolk would be dry on Earth, but it was savory. The yolk has a texture similar to custard, and the whole thing was almost like a pastry dessert. It was surprisingly pleasant. *If Earth eggs tasted this good, I would probably eat them daily.*

"Oh, my, that's good. Is this a normal Willorian chicken egg?" I ask, verifying.

"Yup! I can show you our hen house later, and we can get them right from the coop. You could eat them at any time. *I feel like my mind will explode at some point with all this new information.*

"Here, have a pastry." She says, handing me one.

"No, that's okay. I'm not a big, sweet person in the morning." *I always hate admitting this because what kid doesn't want to have sweets in the morning? Right?*

She gives me a confused stare.

"I get headaches due to consuming sugar too early," I tell her.

"Well, try it anyway. You might be surprised."

"Okay..."

Grabbing hold of the pastry, I take a small bite. Whoa! My mind is blown. "What is this?"

"They're called memorpasteries."

"Memorpastries?" I question.

"Memorpastries. They have a tiny bit of magic in them. When you take a bite, they connect to memories or thoughts. So, with you wanting something less sugary and maybe more substantial or with protein, the pastry's magic created a pastry just for you!"

That's amazing! I take another bite and then shove the whole thing in my mouth. The second bite tastes like a bagel, but then when I ate the entire thing, it provided a glorious array of memories from Mom and me picking up doughnuts at the local bakery before her work shift, to her baking me a cake, to her famous Pain au Chocolat, or chocolate croissants. A tear drifts down my cheek as my memory flashes back to the day, *the day after Dad left for the first time and was going to be gone for a month at a time. Mom let me stay home from school as she called in sick to work. We slept in, played games, and baked. She has a knack for baking but doesn't get to use it often with her job. She made her specialty, and we enjoyed it fresh from the oven.*

"Whoa, are you okay?" Echo interjects, snapping me out of my memory.

Shaking my head, I clear my throat and tell her about my flashback.

"Aw, Aidan, I know how much you miss her. Now that things have calmed down for a bit, we can try to message her today.

"What? Are you serious? Why haven't we done that yet?" I spill out the questions.

"Yes, sorry. With everything going on, I didn't want to pile on another thing, but since things have quieted down, we can plan on doing that today. With our mail and Earth's, it will take a while for her to get the letter because of the Nexus and finding the right person who has the power to pass through since no one knows how to find a Ripple." she says, chuckling to herself.

"A Ripple?" I ask.

"Yes, Ripples are essentially portals, but rare. There have only been a handful of Ripples over the last few years. Many

Unnaturals have been trying to discover how these particular portals work, but no one truly knows. Our more popular portals are called Nexuses and they'recreated by the Travelers. These Unnaturals are the ones who harness the ability to take hold of the power and allow other Unnaturals to pass through. These portals connect to other realms nearby and far away, and even Earth, though not many Unnaturals travel to Earth anymore, and you need special permission to go. Let's focus on getting the letter out today, and then we will tackle the next challenge later."

"Okay!" I say vigorously, nodding my head.

Chuckling, I try to change the topic, "So... what about bacon? Is there something different about that?"

She laughs, "No...no, that is normal."

20

Art Knowledge Coming In Hot!

Breakfast was unlike anything I've ever tasted. It was amazing, to say the least. If this is breakfast, I want to see what lunch and dinner look like.

After breakfast, Echo told me I could head back to my room and relax while she took care of some things. She said she would meet up with me after doing some work. I'm not sure what work she has to do, but she said she would find me later to catch up.

Unsure where else to go, I head to my room. Upon entering my room, I plop down on my bed, staring at the posters hanging on the room's wall as my mind drifts. I think about what Echo told me earlier, actually, a few days ago now, how everything changes at night. I will have to see what she meant tonight. I grab my sketchbook, remembering it had dropped earlier. Grabbing its thick leather cover, I glance over the pages, flipping past my face. Next time we're in town - if there is a town here- I'll need to pick up another sketchbook to add to my growing stack at home.

Pausing when a drawing catches my attention. I quickly turn

the pages back to where my attention was fixated on. The line work is faint as if it were hastily sketched, and it could be easily erased with a swipe of a palm, and its fate forever changed. Analyzing the drawing, I make out six, no seven, dragon scales, all displaying different markings on their surface. Some have straight lines running horizontally, some vertically, and some have curved lines. Resembling how a child draws the waves of an ocean running across its surface.

Grabbing my pencils, I take out the B graphite pencil shade and go over each dragon scale's faint lines. When I initially drew it, I must have used the 2H graphite pencil shade. Once I have reviewed all the dragon scales and their surfaces, I push my sketchbook arm's-length away to assess it. Out of the seven dragon scales, I notice the scale with the wavy lines has kept the 2H graphite shade. Pulling the sketchbook toward my body, I go over the lines again with the 2B graphite shade, but nothing happens. Nothing! There is no change. My eyes dart to the others on the page to see if they are holding the B graphite shade. Are they? *Interesting!*

Curiosity still fills my head with the wavy and faint lines on the scale as I decide to walk to clear my head. Grabbing my backpack, filled with my sketchbook and sword, I sling it over my shoulder and head out the door. Once outside my bedroom, I look down at each end of the hall, unsure where to go. Hearing some chatter down the hall to my left, I choose to go in that direction. Walking down the hall, I look around, noticing this place is enormous! There are three more levels above me and nearly twenty rooms on each side of the building. *This building didn't look this big from the outside. It must be using some magic to enhance its size.*

A sound catches me off guard. Listening more closely, it

reverberates like pellets or hail hitting a vehicle's windshield. Instinct takes over, and I drop to a crouch, looking all around for the source, afraid I will be hit with whatever is falling. I realize we're not getting pounded with hail when a small boy appears in front of me with blond hair, dull blue eyes, and...elf-like ears. He crouches down next to me. He crouches down next to me and goes to grab my hand, only for his long talons to seize my hand instead. He looks at me softly, then with his other free hand, one long talon rises, pointing to the sky. Looking between his talons and dull blue eyes, I see his eyes are moving upward in the same direction as his talons. Following his direction, I look up and am relieved to understand what I'm hearing finally. I see the sky isn't the sky at all, it's a glass ceiling; and rain is pelting against the glass, echoing all around. Relief washes over every part of my body. Smiling back down at the boy, I see he has released my hand and is getting up to leave. I reach to stop him, just as he slowly turns and waves with his talon fingers, and then he's gone.

21

Ghostly Pale to Black.

Walking further down the hall, with the rain still hitting the glass ceiling, I come across a large banquet room. Instead of the traditional tables and chairs, this room is filled with long tables reminiscent of those in a library. The chairs range from comfortable to ones as stiff as a tree—no, really, some are actually made from a tree trunk. Bookshelves surround the room, filled with books, vases, and small trinkets. In the far corner sits an oversized leather chair with a three-foot wooden table sitting beyond the leather. It seems like the perfect spot to sit and think. Without a second thought, I head over and plop down into its massive frame. The chair's back is enormous in comparison to my body, but once I settle in, I pull out my sketchbook, pencils, and sword. Laying the sword at the edge of the table, I find a blank page and start to sketch the sword in front of me. I make sure to capture the intricate details of the hilt.

As my pencil starts to create the pommel at the end of the hilt, I notice it's different from the usual metal. Grabbing the hilt, I feel the cold metal touch my skin, sending shivers down my spine. The pommel is almost shimmering, and reflective, and not a circle but more of a teardrop shape. Looking more closely at the center, it appears to be a dragon scale.

Without warning, a body sits down where I had initially placed the sword on the table. Startled, I glance up toward the figure sitting in front of me, and see she's in a new set of clothes. She is wearing a pair of ripped jeans, a light blue tank top, and a jean jacket. She has combed out her hair and it's no longer frizzy. Now it's long and sleek.

"What are you up to?" Echo asks.

"Drawing," I replied quickly, still focused on my sword's pommel, as my pencils seemed to be moving on their own.

"Ah, I got a little nervous when I didn't see you in your room a few minutes ago. Figured you must have gone out to explore."

"Yeah, I got bored, especially since there isn't much to do here."

"Makes sense," she chuckles. "Hey, is that a new drawing?" She looks down at my sketchbook.

"Yeah, I just drew it a few minutes ago. I'm still working on the shading, but I wanted to sketch my sword. It's not finished yet, but check this out!" I pass my sword toward her, pointing specifically to the hilt, especially the pommel.

"Whoa! Is that a dragon scale?" She asks.

"I think so, but I have no idea how it got there or how it was made. I did some research and learned that pommels—-the end part of the sword," I say, pointing to it again "are usually made out of iron, an alloy, bronze, and some can be made out of bone. I guess dragon scales wouldn't be too much different."

"I guess not. You mentioned someone gave you this sword?"

"Yes, a mystery figure. Why?"

"Just curious, but it's too bad you can't ask him where he

got this, especially if it's a true dragon. The ones I've heard of are the magic dragon scales. I wondered if it would be rock-shaped and painted to look like a dragon scale. I don't know, though."

"Interesting. I didn't think of that."

We sit in silence for a few short moments, staring at the possible dragon scale.

"Anyway, did you finish your work?" I ask, breaking the silence.

"Yup! All done, at least for now."

"What did you have to do?"

"Just paperwork, mainly. I won't bother you with boring stuff."

"Okay. Hey, I have a question."

"Shoot!"

"I've been meaning to ask you for a while but keep talking myself out of it."

Echo cuts me off, "just ask the question." she replies with a chuckle.

Taking a deep breath, "Okay, three years ago, by chance, did you crash into a set of lockers at a school, justs for a second, and then vanish?"

She thinks for a long moment. I feel awkward staring at her while she thinks. Refocusing my eyes, I bring them to my sword while she ponders. When she speaks again, my eyes shoot up to meet hers.

"Yes..." she pauses again. "I didn't know where I landed, but after I hit something, I heard a loud shriek. Wait, was that you?"

I feel my cheeks redden, especially the still-swollen ones. "I didn't think I screamed that loud." I lied.

"Yes! That was you, and you screamed like a little girl!"

"Anyone would have screamed if a random body came flying out of nowhere, hit the lockers next to them and then suddenly disappeared."

She bursts into laughter. After a few minutes of laughing, she clears her throat and starts up again. "Ha, yes, I remember that day. Oof, that was not a fun one."

"How so?" Now I'm confused and curious.

Shaking her head to clear her mind, but before she says another word, her eyes widen, reaching over and abruptly grabs hold of my sketchbook.

"Aidan?" she says, sounding panicky. "Did… did you write this?" She asks while pointing at the bottom of the page.

I glance toward where she is pointing. It looks to be cross-hatching. I don't have any recall of recently drawing that, but maybe I did when I was talking with Echo.

"Maybe," I say unconvincingly. Her face goes pale.

"What is it? I ask. I wonder if I was doodling when we were talking.

She starts to open her mouth to speak when a knock comes from near the door, well, actually the metal door frame itself. A tall woman starts walking into the room toward us. I can't make out her features until she is almost in front of me. It… no, it can't be…

"Aidan, this is Gaelica."

No, no, her name is not Gaelica. *Flashes of her pass through my memories, helping me over the years, helping me read when teachers sent me to the office for "disturbing the class." When I get caught up in my drawings, she'd make sure I didn't miss too much of my classes. She wrote me passes to excuse me from being late, due to another teacher. She's the one person at that horrible school who noticed. I disappeared for three days, and no student or any teachers noticed. It's Janice! Janice, my school's receptionist, but...but wait. What is she doing here?*

"Aidan, are you okay? You look like you've seen a ghost." Echo interrupts my memories.

"Hi, Aidan. It's been some time since I've seen you." Janice tells me in a cheerful voice.

"What?" I stammered. But before I can comprehend what was happening, my vision starts to blur and then everything goes black.

Illustration drawn by Tina Bartlett

22

Her History or Mine?

I'm not sure how much time has passed–minutes or hours–but when I blink my eyes open, Echo is pressing a cold washcloth to my forehead, and she holds a bag of ice, presumably for my bruise or maybe there's a new one. *I never did apply ice to the bruise, a dumb move on my part.* Echo lets out a loud sigh of relief, removing the washcloth and ice.

"Aidan, you're awake! You passed out," she shrieks.

"Sorry, I don't know what happened," I admit.

"Aidan," a soft voice behind Echo calls to me.

Shooting straight up into a seated position, I let the events flood my brain before I passed out. Janice, my school receptionist, is here in Willorian. She was the one person from my school who cared about me, probably the only reason I don't have a thick file on hand for the outrageous number of times I was sent to the office for "class disturbance."

"Janice…" I stammer. "Is that really you?"

"Aidan, no, I think you have her confused with someone else, this is Gaelica," Echo softly shares with me.

Janice places a hand on Echo's shoulder. "No, Echo, he's

right. He knows me as Janice, his school receptionist."

Echo looks shocked as her mouth gapes open just a tad.

"She...she helped me when teachers at my school didn't. Most sent me to the office when they thought I was making fun of the class or their work, but in truth, I was struggling with reading. Janice was my savior in the office. She would let me hang out with her for a few minutes to an hour and then send me back to class with a note," I explain to Echo.

"Yup! You were caught 'doodling' in class and not paying attention," Janice says with a chuckle and her fingers motioning mid-air quotations. "Then when teachers would call on you, you would struggle, and they didn't care, nor did they take the time to help you," she adds with a spiteful tone.

"No one at the school liked me besides Janice," I chirp, yet somber.

Her smile is genuine, but then it changes, becoming sour as if she remembers something she forgot to tell me.

"Aidan," she starts, "there's something I need to tell you."

"Okay," I say nervously.

Janice and Echo glance at each other as if they are talking without speaking. When Echo nods, Janice grabs a chair from a table next to ours and takes a seat near me. Echo takes her seat again on top of the table, next to my sword.

Instead of Janice starting, Echo does. "Remember when we were younger, I told you I would come with my Dad as he traveled through town, and that's when I met you."

"Yeah..."

"Well, the truth is," she takes a deep breath. "I don't know who my Dad is."

What?

"I was on a mission. Well, I was supposed to be, but the last time I saw you, I messed up. I was supposed to be doing an assignment, but instead, I was hanging out with an Earth boy and missed my target. That Earth boy was you, and when the Elders found out, my access to Earth was revoked."

A dozen questions flood my mind. "Mission? Target? Does she have access?"

"Okay," I start, but Echo cuts me off and continues.

"A handful of years ago, Willorian relics started disappearing. These relics may have little to no significance to us—the Unnaturals—but they were originally contained in Willorian, in the House. Unfortunately, some made their way to Earth and other realms. We have no knowledge of how the relics found their way to Earth, but the Elders sent two chosen Unnaturals, myself being one of them due to my ability to astral project and teleport."

"But, I thought you only recently learned how to astral project?" I say, cutting in.

Janice sends a scowl my way for interrupting the story. "Yes, Echo is refining her abilities now, but she knew how to do it at a very young age, she was the best." Janice states.

"Was?" I asked, confused.

Janice takes a deep breath. "Echo was supposed to meet with a buyer."

Echo chimes in, "The day I met you was when I was supposed to meet with a buyer. A rare relic that held more power than a relic should have. Willorian magic can be valuable to Earthlings if they knew how to harness it. We heard rumors about this buyer and the information he had about who took it and other relics from Willorian, including who specifically sold it to him. But since I was late to the meeting, I missed my opportunity and the information we all desperately needed."

Echo slowly finishes.

My mind flashes back to that day, the last day I saw Echo. I had a hard day at school, and when we first met by the tree, I was quiet and hiding in my comics. She got me to talk, and when she heard that two boys picked on me today at school, she went to take care of it. She told me to wait and that she'd be back. When she returned, close to an hour later, her hands were in rough shape. Dried blood coated a few of her knuckles. When I questioned her about what happened, she told me not to worry about it—they shouldn't be messing with me after that. And they didn't, but their friends did. They started to mess with me to no end. I was never able to tell her or even thank her for trying because I never saw her after that day. I wondered if she got caught or arrested for what she had done and was the reason I never saw her again.

Janice cleared her throat. "When Echo returned back empty-handed and without words, word spread that she had failed, missing both the target and the meeting. The Elders were furious. She never told them what really happened, but later, she confided in me. She told me about you and how you were different— that you struggled more than most to read and understand English, which is why you drew everything instead. She told me where to find you at Prairieland Middle School.

"I wasn't sure how I was going to introduce myself to you, but I saw they were hiring a receptionist, so I decided that would be my first step. I began to work on a plan to find you, maybe to call you to the office, but what would the reason be? Then, one day, you were sent to the office for disturbance in class." I had my suspicions, but since I didn't know what you looked like, I waited."

When you started attempting to work on your homework

and struggled, I knew I was close. Then, one day, while you were in the office, your backpack spilled over when you headed to the bathroom, and while I was cleaning it up, I saw your sketchbook. There was a page tabbed as though you were coming back to finish it later. The drawing was of a multicolored sky above a forest. To any individual, your drawing would have looked like any forest or wooded area, but to me, I could tell you were already drawing a Willorian landscape without even knowing it.

As you moved up in grades, I grew more nervous about how to tell you everything—about me, Willorian, and even about yourself. But, when you continued to get into 'trouble' and were sent to the office. I continued to put it off. Disappointed in myself, I knew I'd eventually have to tell you, but when you didn't show up to school for a few days, I knew I was too late. I returned to Willorian, only to find out you had already been there.."

I cut her off abruptly, "So, this whole time, you were spying on me!" I'm practically screaming. My face is red with fire.

"No...No, not exactly. I don't know if I would officially call it that. More like looking out for you. Each time you were sent to the office, I feared one day they might expel you, but thankfully, we never crossed that bridge. One of the days you were called into the office, I had brought in a Willorian History textbook, and I decided to test out a theory I had. I spread out the book in front of you, telling you it was a family heirloom, and I was trying to decipher it. With one look at the text, you started reading it flawlessly, no sign of the reading struggles you usually had. That's when I confirmed my suspicions of you. You were an Unnatural from Willorian."

"As the months went on, I kept a close eye on you, trying

to figure out your power. Unnaturals' abilities are obvious, while others remain hidden. But you never showed any signs of power—until recently," she explains. She explains.

"Wait, what gifts are noticeable?" I interrupt her, asking possibly the least important question.

"Some Unnaturals have the ability to lift heavy objects—cars or fallen trees—without even realizing it. They'll casually pick up a table or a stack of chains as if it's a piece of paper. Others might have fire abilities, and they'll accidentally start a fire in class, in a place where fire shouldn't be allowed. More hidden powers include plant menders or mind readers. These abilities are subtle at first; they don't know what they're doing, but eventually, they catch on—especially if they have been around magic or Willorian their entire lives. Unlike you."

We all sit in silence until one question looms in my mind.

"So Echo," I break the silence, "When I met you and Calix, he mentioned you were still learning your powers, but Janice said you had full power before. How is that possible?"

"I was wondering when you would catch on," she says, grinning. "That day, the last day I saw you, I missed my meeting."

"Was that the day you...you took care of my bullies?" I question cutting off her story.

She only nods. "The Elders gave me a choice: either lose my magic entirely or start over—relearn everything from scratch. Most would choose to lose it altogether because of how painful and tedious the process is. Some can't bear the thought of having to re-experience it all. But..." She pauses, her voice faltering as the weight of the memory hits her. "I chose to restart. I couldn't imagine a world where I didn't have my powers."

"She actually restored her powers faster than someone learning them for the first time," Janice chimes in.

23

Drawing or Writing?

I sit there in silence, attempting to absorb the information overload that Echo and Janice just dropped on me. I see Echo trying to talk to me, her words moving, but no sound escapes them. I feel numb and empty as if my whole life has been a lie. Everything rushes past me, not in words that flew from their mouths but in pictures. My mind is racing, pictures playing in videos.

A rushing sound, like water crashing down a waterfall, travels through my ears, pulling me back to the present.

"Aidan...Aidan? Are you with us?" Janice asks, reaching to grab my hand. I pull it away before she can make contact.

"You...you both lied to me," I stammer, still shocked.

"No, Aidan," Echo starts.

"Well, yes, we did," Janice cuts in, "but it was to protect you."

"NO! Everyone says they're trying to protect me when they're only hiding things... important things. Everyone's afraid I won't be able to handle it. I'm old enough to handle it!" I shout back at them. Goosebumps line my arms as my face draws in heat. Abruptly standing, I start grabbing everything off the table, shoving it into my backpack. When I go to close the book, I hear Janice gasp.

"Aidan! Stop!" She grabs hold of my sketchbook before I can shove it into my backpack.

Looking down at my sketch, still on the page of my sword, she flips the book upside down, and that's when I notice she's looking at the same crosshatch marks Echo was examining before.

"Aidan, when did you write this?" Janice repeats Echo's original question. Running her fingers along the lines.

"Yes, as I told Echo when she asked, I don't remember drawing it, but I was doodling when Echo and I were talking earlier. I figured it was some crosshatching."

"No, no…" she pauses, "these are no crosshatches. These are words," Janice stammers out.

Words? How?

Looking more intently at the sketch, it's as if my mind clears from a fog covering my eyes.

"What does it mean?" I ask again, but there is no one in particular.

"I'm not sure. Janice, do you know?" Echo asks, looking toward Janice.

"We are not prepared for what's coming," Janice mutters.

24

The Messages?

"What do you mean we are not prepared for what's coming?" Echo softly asks Janice. "Can you explain what this means?"

Janice takes another look at the *words.* "Yes, though I haven't seen this writing since I was young. This is an old language, like the start of Willorian time, old. It hasn't been used in a few hundred years. Not many know, let alone understand, this language."

Echo's eyes widened to the size of saucers.

Janice studies the words again. "Okay, see right here." She points to what looks to be a '+' with two dots on the right side. "This means 'Fight.' Next, it looks like a cross, symbolizing two swords with a dot between them that means 'War.' Then here, what looks like a capital 'I' with a dot above it means 'Win.' The half-circle with a line and dot can either mean 'Lose' or 'Death.' So together it means 'Fight, War, Win, or Lose/Death.'"

"How do you know this language, Aidan?" Echo asks.

"I...I don't," I stammer, "I've never seen it before. Wait...I have seen this before, not exactly these words." Pausing we all fall silent as we try to make sense of the symbols. Then, *suddenly*, realization hits me. "But with the symbols mixed together, in a different order, I definitely have!" I say, starting to get excited.

"What do you mean?" Echo asks.

"My History paper. I turned it in feeling confident, but when my teacher handed it back to me, these symbols covered the entire thing. It was as if I had written my entire assignment in these symbols. He allowed me to redo it, but I never got the chance. The weird thing was, when I turned it in, I distinctly remember it being written in English, but when I got it back, it was in these symbols." I explain.

"Aidan," Janice starts, but before she can say more, a package—the size of a mini-cooler— falls from the ceiling, seemingly out of nowhere, crashing through the ceiling tiles and landing directly onto the table. I jerk back, pushing myself and the chair backward, as Echo leaps clear off the table, stumbling to catch her balance, while Janice springs out of her chair, knocking it over.

After a moment of all of us staring at it and catching our shocked breaths, I take a hesitant step closer to the table and glance at the shipping label.

```
From:
To: Aidan
```

"What the…?" is all I can manage to utter as I start to reach for the box.

"Aidan, don't open it. We don't know what's inside." Janice says, worried.

"It's addressed to me. It can't be bad, right?"

"Who knows you're here? No one should know."

I think about that for a moment. *Who knows, I'm in Willorian? The only people I know are Echo, Janice, and Calix (but I doubt he'd send me a package unless it's a magical fist to punch me again.) I can't think of anyone else who knows I'm here.*

"Do you want to help me open it?" Echo asks. I look at Janice for confirmation.

Echo looks nervous but nods. She reaches into her pocket and pulls out a pocket knife. Slowly, she slices the tape on the package. When the knife cuts the last bit of tape, we all step back, holding our collective breath, unsure what is about to emerge from the box. When nothing happens, I slowly pull the box tabs open and look inside.

There's something glistening between the sheets of tissue paper. Once everything is carefully pulled out— Janice and Echo gasp in unison when they see what's wrapped up in the tissue paper. Unfolding what remains covered, I hold in both hands two halves of a dragon scale. The dragon scale is covered in wavy lines, similar to my drawing from earlier, where the lines wouldn't darken. A memory tickles the back of my mind, the lines on my drawing wouldn't darken because the dragon scale was broken, and somehow, my drawing *knew* that to be true.

Beneath the dragon scale, nestled in the box, lies a scroll, curled and bound with a ribbon. I hand one half of the scale to Janice and the other to Echo, then reach for the scroll. Unfurling it, I read aloud the hastily scribbled words on the fragile parchment:

"We must return. Restore the balance of the world and magic."

25

Random Doorknobs?

Chaos erupts around me. I can't help but re-read the message on the scroll over and over, my words forming on my lips. I can hear Janice and Echo muttering to each other. When Janice starts frantically checking her pockets, I only lift my gaze meeting their eyes. After a tense moment, she finds what she was searching for and pulls out a handheld device similar to a cellphone. Her fingers fly over it with great speed. I fear smoke and fire will fly out of her fingers.

"It's done," Janice plainly states after a few more tappings.

"What's done?" I asked.

"Echo, can you please prepare everyone?" She asks, ignoring my question.

"Prepare who for what?" I ask again.

"Yes!" Echo responds.

"Alright, I'll prepare Aidan, and we will meet in the center square in a day's time. Everyone will be there."

Echo nods in response. Then, to my surprise, Echo blinks, and she's gone. Assuming she has transported herself to another location, I turn and gawk at Janice. "Can you please, for the love of this world, tell me what's going on?"

"Yes...yes," she mutters under her breath, "I will, but I'll need to tell you along the way. Grab your things, and we need to go now!"

Scrambling to gather what's left on the table—my sword, backpack, and sketchbook—I race out of the room to catch up with her. By the time I reach the hallway, she's already standing at its center. Out of breath, I implore once more, "What is happening?"

"We need to get supplies for you and then meet up with Echo and everyone else."

"Supplies for what? Who's everyone else?"

She abruptly stops and turns, her eyes locking with mine. "There is a war about to be unleashed in Willorian. For some reason, whoever or whatever is about to start it seems to like you enough to give you a warning. We suspect the one initiating this war intends to recreate or change the way magic is dispersed. When the War of All Wars broke out between the Unnatural and the Creatures, it was unsettling. No one knew what would happen. Even our high-level Seeker saw two different outcomes, no one could predict what would happen." She pauses briefly and continues on her face-walking trek, scrambling to catch up. I realize one of my shoelaces is untied. I fear if I stop to fix it, Janice will leave me in the dust.

"Now," she starts up again, "we are dealing with someone who wants to rebalance magic. Whoever is doing this must be immensely powerful to send us this," she holds up the scroll. "And powerful enough to take on all the Creatures and Unnaturals in Willorian if their plan doesn't go the way they hope. But before all that can begin, we need to get you fitted for some gear in case another war breaks out and you don't have anything to protect you with. Follow me."

I'm stunned into silence for most of the way out of the main hallway. It isn't until my name is sounded multiple times that I snap out of my stupor and catch up. We have passed every room on the main floor and are now heading toward the back of the building. After passing through a small, narrow hallway, where even Janice has to crouch down, a door appears. Janice shoves her hand into her front coat pocket and pulls out an old skeleton key. Sliding the key into its keyhole, we wait until we hear the click of metal connecting. *The last time I saw an active skeleton key, the keyhole was in my grandmother's house before they had to move to an assisted living. I remember when I would collect them all and run around trying to rematch them. Mom and Dad weren't thrilled with it, but Grandma and I had a blast!*

Once the key makes its connection, Janice turns the iron doorknob and pushes the door open. Her arm outstretched, indicating I should proceed first. I take a small, hesitant step before I hear the door click behind me. Janice is half a step behind me. As we continue down the hallway, I had originally assumed this led to the basement. It turns out it's more reminiscent to an old castle hallway heading toward the dungeon. Bricks and a lantern lie against the cool, damp walls every few feet. The ground is concrete but damp, and roughly every tenth step, there seems to be a random doorknob resting in the walls, not attached to any door–just a doorknob in the middle of the concrete. *Weird, but maybe not the weirdest thing I've seen yet.*

We continue down the long hallway—the concrete below our feet has turned to dirt and stones. If we were in a massive basement with multiple corridors, I would assume we were lost, but there's only one direction to go–straight.

Finally, at the end of the hallway, we pause. Stealing a glance up at Janice, I can barely make out her facial expression in the flickering light of a nearby lantern. She pulls out the same device she had earlier and points it at the wall in front of us. A few beeps emit from the device just as a flash of blinding light shines from the wall. I shield my eyes, allowing them to adjust to the sudden brightness when the light fades, not completely gone, just more tolerable to look at. Janice puts the device back into her pocket and places her hands on the bricks in front of us.

At first glance, I would have assumed she was trying to push the brick wall inward, but that's not the case. When the palms of her hands make contact with the wall, they start to glow. I take a nervous step back, tripping over my shoelace, and crash to the ground. My hands brace my fall but landed in a dirty puddle. Janice doesn't look back at me or seem to have heard me. Her focus is on her hands and the wall, which is now turning into a door. A door frame is being drawn out as if a marker was drawing the outline before our eyes. I can tell she is getting weak due to the strenuous effort as the light on her palms starts to dim. The door completes its path and creaks open.

Sunlight peeks around the cracks of the door's outline. As Janice regains her balance and composure, she swings around to see me lying on the wet and rocky floor.

"What are you doing on the ground?" She asks.

"I tripped and fell," I tell her bluntly.

"Well, get up. We need to get you ready," she says, reaching down to offer her hand.

Once I'm on my feet, Janice looks at me, "You ready?"

"Ready for what?" I question
"Everything to change," she trembles.

26

Earth Runts?

Janice continues to push the brick door open, revealing a secret behind the flood of sunlight pouring in. I shield my eyes with my hand again, trying to see past the rays of light. When the burst of light subsides, I see... a new world.

The door must be magic. That's the only explanation I can think of. One minute, we are in a dark, damp concrete hallway with brick walls and mysterious doorknobs. The next, we are in a village. Houses and shops line each side of the road, their roofs steep, and their stalls are filled with fresh fruit and small trinkets. In the distance, a blacksmith hammers against metal as the air's filled with animal manure mixed with the scent of freshly baked bread and pastries. I spin around, trying to take everything in at once.

When a movement catches my attention behind a set of plants, it halts my spinning attention. I center my attention on its leaves beginning to shake. I don't realize what I'm doing until my feet start to move toward the movement. My eyes are still fixed on the plant, and its leaves are shaking. A small, high-pitched noise emits from whatever is behind the plant. I abruptly stop, listening very closely, only able to hear my heart beating in my ears, as my stomach begins to turn. The noise resembles a small whimper, then a chewing sound. Reaching out a shaking hand, I pull down some of the branches, feeling the twigs under the soft leaves poke at my skin. I pull back when one branch cuts my skin, leaving a small red line along my finger. Thorns.

I never understood why some plants, especially flowers, contain thorns. One summer, Mom decided to plant some roses on the patio and when it was time to pick them, I wrapped my hand around the stem, only to immediately pull back in time to see multiple thorns sticking out of my hand and blood streaming down my arm. Mom had to pull out each thorn and clean me up. My hand was wrapped with cloth for a week, letting the wounds heal.

Another sound pulls me out of my memory and back to the thorny bush in front of me. The bush is now growling. I don't move quickly enough before I am stumbling backward and falling to the ground once again. Looking around, I frantically search for the growling plant, afraid whatever it was would attack me while I was down. Though the plant is no longer in front of me, instead, there's a...wait...what? It's a puppy covered in plant stems and greenery. I can make out its tail wagging with excitement as a pale pink tongue hangs from its flower head.

Before I get the chance to react and play with the weird pup, I heard my name yelled out, but was unable to detect who called me. My head whips back and forth from behind me to in front of me. I see a few townspeople and Janice running for me, but everything is a blur. My mind is racing. *Were they afraid the puppy would attack or lick me to death?* Glancing back at the puppy, I realize why everyone was rushing toward me, the puppy is no longer a puppy. He has grown five times his original size, his head now enormous,his mouth open, ready to devour me and the whole town. I can see his eyes are bright and large, with only the thought of *lunch* on his mind.

"Aidan!" I hear my name once again. "Back up slowly, and do not make any sudden movements."

"O..Okay," I croak out. Still in my fallen position, I slowly rise to my feet, watching the dog's eyes follow me as I rise. Shuffling my feet backward, I begin my slow trek back toward Janice when there's a sudden movement in the back of the dog's throat, which starts to glow.

"AIDAN! Get down!" Jancie shouts, hearing her but not seeing her and the other townsfolk flattening to the ground.

My eyes are glued to the dog's mouth or, more importantly, the glowing object in its throat. There's fire filling the dog's mouth. Fearing for my life, I start to scramble backward only to hear "DOWN!" Again.

With a flick of the wind, the dog not only stops the fire growing from his mouth but, in fact, lies down. Shooting my head back to the crowd, a young boy raises his hands upward and continues giving the dog directions, but I am unable to hear or understand them. My mind is clouded.

"Aidan, come here," Janice calls out to me. I feel my body move towards her, and it isn't until her hand grips around my arm that I am drawn from the clouds.

"Didn't your school teach you?"

"I don't know, maybe I got sent to the office during that lecture," I say, letting out a small chuckle.

She shakes her head, still gripping my arm. "Come. We have an appointment." As though I wasn't about to be fried by a fire-breathing dog.

Janice pulls me down the alley of the village toward a small makeshift storefront. As we push through the front door, a small bell rings out above the door. A small elderly woman comes out of the back room holding a pair of round glasses. She walks hunched over and slow.

"Hello, we have an appointment," Janice tells the old lady.

"An appointment..." she scoffs. "I haven't had one of those scheduled in...I don't know, maybe ten years."

"It's for Willorian"

"Yeah, yeah..." she waves her hand. "Willorian!" She scoffs.

"What? Willorian gives you guys magic." Janice informs her.

"Magic? What magic? We were given a sliver of magic, barely enough to do laundry with. The community here has come together and agreed that we're saving that magic for *emergencies*, but the pup out there has a sweet tooth for magic and devoured it. Now, he's the only powerful thing here. We're just as powerless as those runts on Earth."

"Runts?" I shout in question. Anger is filling my veins.

"Yes... runts. People who have no knowledge of magic, and even if they did have any, wouldn't know how to use it if it came with an instruction manual." She spits out, spittle flying from her mouth.

"Earth people are great, and yes, we might not have magic, but we are taught to believe there is magic. Especially in the *real* world! You need to harness the *magic* of anything coming your way because if you were given magic all the time, we would lose sight of the real magic— how it's not guaranteed all the time." I'm shouting at this point. I didn't realize it until I finish and see a crowd of people around the entrance of the old woman's shop. At the end of my *"speech,"* or maybe it was more of a rant, I see others nodding and murmuring to one another.

The old lady looks between Janice and me. "Is he okay?" She asks, pointing to me over her shoulder.

"He's from Earth. He was an Earth *runt*, as you called him, until recently," Janice informs her.

I'm heaving with exhaustion. I'm not sure why, but explaining or maybe the yelling took a lot of energy out of me.

Glancing between Janice, the old lady, and the crowd has gathered, I nod and state, "Didn't we have an appointment?" I clear my throat.

Janice nods. "Yes, we need a fitting for Aidan here, for war clothes."

The older lady looks grimly at me, then back at Janice. "You will have to wait."

"But..." Janice interrupts.

"Wait, because I have another order to do ahead of yours. Go get yourself something to eat, or something for him. He's too skinny." She points toward me with her wrinkled finger.

"Fine, we will be back in thirty minutes. This is urgent, so please hurry up." Janice tells the old lady.

"Yeah, yeah," the older lady says, dismissively waving her hand as she shuffles to the back once more.

27

German Is Hard.

Janice and I exit the clothing shop, staring out into the open. I try to take everything in. I feel as though I am back in time. There are no cars, only horses and wagons, people wearing cloaks, swords being made, and a house on the hill behind the shops is guarded by fence, with sheep grazing in the grass. *I wonder if they have plumbing here, c*huckling to myself.

"Are you hungry?" Janice inquires.

"Yes!"

"Perfect, let's go!"

We head toward a small tavern. Big, muscled men are sitting on the porch, drinking what appears to be beer. *It can't be much later than lunchtime Can it?* Upon entering through the creaky wooden door, everyone silences their conversations and glances in our direction.

I freeze, unsure of what to do. It isn't until I see Janice heading toward an open table that I step out of my frozen state and follow her.

"How may I help you?" A waiter asks in a sly tone.

"Could we get some menus, please?" Janice asks.

He pulls out two small rectangular menus and places them on the table. "I'll bring out water." With that, he turns around and leaves.

"Why is everyone staring at us?" I whisper to Janice.

"We're from Willorian. We have magic, and they can sense it."

"Are we no longer in Willorian?"

"Technically, no, we're in Lavina."

"Lavina? Where's that?"

"Lavina is another realm connected to Willorian. We've been connected to them for many generations, and when the Elders changed magic's fate, we gave them magic to help their people." She leans in closer. "I will tell you a secret. You must not divulge it, promise me."

"I promise," I say.

She looks around, leaning in closer. "I don't know for certain, but I heard the Elders placed two magic relics that provide powerful magic throughout Lavina by their Elders. But now it worries me that they have no magic. I wonder if the same thing is happening to Lavina as it happens in Willorian. If it is, we may also have to prepare for a fight against Lavina." She pulls away as our waiter comes back, bringing our water.

"Have we decided on food yet?" He asks in a rush.

"No, we'll need a few more minutes." Janice rebuts.

With a huff, the waiter leaves.

"If Lavina's magic relics have been taken or disappeared, why is everyone looking at us?" I ask.

"They believe all Willorian Creatures and Unnaturals are the same and that we want *our* power back. If what the seamstress says is true and their magic is gone, then that means someone or something has found their relic."

"Can I ask a stupid question?" I ask Janice after a long pause.

"Of course!" she says, grabbing her water from the table.

"Are dragons real?"

She freezes, her glass halfway up to her mouth. "What?"

"We have dragon scales, so are dragons real?"

"Oh..." she says, with a small laugh. "No, no, they're not. There hasn't been a sighting of one in... well, let's see, at least a couple thousand years."

"Then how did we acquire dragon scales to put magic into?"

"You know, I don't fully understand it, but an Unnatural collected the scales after the last dragon died. Their essence—the scales—were stored in a Gathering Box, a box for magical items to be protected–until a group of Elders decided to use those dragon scales to disperse magic throughout Willorian."

I nod my head, listening.

The waiter comes back, and Janice places an order. I have yet to look at the menu, so when the waiter turns toward me for my order, I feel my face flush. I take a quick glance down at the menu and read off the first thing I see.

"I will take the Onion Bacon Pie Zweebe." I have no clue how to say the last word, Zwieblkuchen. I feel my face start to flush, and I'm sure it's as red as a tomato right now. Instead of making myself look bad or even worse, I just point to the picture I see. "I will take this, please."

The waiter scribbles down my order and Janice's. *Did she even open her menu?*

I let out a sigh of relief after he leaves.

"Ha, you don't know your German at all, do you?" Janice asks, chuckling behind her water glass.

"Never had to learn German, so nope, not at all."

28

Janice is a What?

The waiter and our food arrive twenty minutes later. Having no idea what I ordered, I find the meal to be delicious. Janice seems to be enjoying her food as well. Out of the blue, Janice starts up a conversation again.

"Hey, before I came back to Willorian, I was still at your high school. The day before I returned, I received a call," she pauses, her soft eyes meeting mine. "It was your mother."

"My Mom?" I exclaimed!

"Yes, she called asking if you had made it to school the last few days. She mentioned she had been working weird hours and didn't see you at home. I was thankful I was the one who answered her call. I told her who I was and that I had heard you were in Willorian."

"What? Does she know what or even where Willorian is?"

"She'd heard about it, but not enough to worry."

"What did she say?"

"We talked for a while. Your Mom filled me in on your Dad coming home from his job and asked where you were. That's when she called the school. She added that the last time you two talked, she had given you his journal, and you asked to read it alone. But, after that, you went for a walk and haven't been home since. She told your Dad not to worry and lied, saying you were working on a project at school. I can tell your Mom doesn't want to worry your Dad while he is at work."

Does Janice not know what my Dad truly does? If my mom were to tell anyone, wouldn't it be Janice, since she's an Unnatural herself who lives in Willorian?

"I told her you would contact her when you are able," Janice continues.

"Do you have a phone or computer I could use to contact her?"

"Sadly, we do not have those here, in Lavina or Willorian."

"You don't have a computer?"

"No..."

"What about a phone?"

"No to that one..."

"How do you contact people in emergencies?" I ask, cutting her off.

"Echo told me you heard a siren's sound a few days ago before she transported you two to the Glass Apartments."

"Yeah, it was either like a screech or a high-pitched siren alarm."

"Well, that was actually...me."

"What?"

"I'm a Babonschee. I report to and call others when bad news is coming. I have a Banshee in my family's line who used to announce death, but now I only report bad news or call for an emergency meeting. I called Willorian to gather everyone to prepare. I knew something was going to happen, just not sure what exactly. Not until you got the package today."

"Do you have a way to communicate with people in other realms?"

"We do, but it's similar to snail mail on Earth."

"How so?"

"You can write a letter, and when someone is granted access to travel through a Nexus, they can carry it with them. The letter is then delivered by whatever means is necessary to ensure it's delivered to the correct person. In each realm, it's different how their mail travels. Some are through animals, some are through mail services like on Earth, and some travel through magic and the wind."

"When can I send one? Can we do it now?" I ask eagerly.

"Let's wait until we get back to Willorian. Then you may write a letter, and we'll try to find someone going through a Nexus to send it with them."

Janice pays the waiter with money that looks to be pink and green. There are no faces or numbers on the money, just a few lines crossing each other with some dots around them, reminding me of the symbols on the scroll. Janice stands before I have a chance to inquire about it.

"Well, it's been more than half an hour. Let's go see if the seamstress has time now."

With that, we leave the tavern and head back to the seamstress's shop.

29

New Wardrobe!

Entering the shop, the small bell rings overhead again, and the old lady waddles out of the back room. "About time you returned," she throws out.

"We wanted to give you plenty of time," Janice replies.

The old lady waves her hand again. "Follow me."

We follow her to the back of the store. Her shop holds everything from small trinkets to endless clothing options. It is perfect for anyone going into a dance or even a battle, with knives and swords everywhere.

Passing through a velvety soft curtain into a large work area, I am surprised by its sheer size. Every type of fabric is hanging on the wall. There are patterns sprawled out on nearly twenty tables. Despite the chaos, each table has tape measures, marking pens, pin cushions, and containers for pens, pencils, and scissors neatly displayed along the edges. I'm gawking at everything when I bump into a hard, rigid body in front of me. Letting out a huff, I look up to see I've run into Janice, who has abruptly stopped to avoid running into the old lady.

"Sorry," I whisper.

"Child, come here," the old lady orders.

"I'm not a child," I tell her.

"You're not an adult. I bet you can't even drive yet."

"I'm sixteen, and I live in the city back home. There's no need to drive."

"City? Back home? Boy, where are you from?"

"Brooklyn," I tell her absently.

"Brooklyn? Is that a new town in Willorian I'm not familiar with?"

"Willorian? No, it's a city in New York, on Earth."

"Earth?" Her eyes shoot up to meet Janice's, as if she didn't make the connection before she sent us away.

"No, it can't be. Is he?" The old lady questions while still staring at Janice.

All Janice does is nod.

"Well!" Her mood does a complete one-eighty. "Let's get you fitted. You are going to need a whole new wardrobe."

—

By the time we finish, I'm exhausted both mentally and physically. I have no idea how many times this woman measured me. *The first five times would have been enough, but there is no chance.*

After the many measurements, she runs around the entire room, grabbing armfuls of fabric with each lap she takes. When she comes back in front of us, she rushes through each one, placing fabric against my skin to match my tone and to see if I liked the fabric. She asks if the material is okay, too itchy, too hot, or not enough warmth, and about twenty more questions afterward.

At one point, Janice reminded the older lady, "We need clothes for a possible war or, more importantly, fighting-style clothing, not clothing for a ball." *I'm really hoping I am not being fitted for ball attire. I know nothing about balls, although I know nothing about fighting and wars, either.*

"You're done. Sit, stand, do whatever. Give me thirty minutes, and your order will be done."

Thirty minutes seemed short for the time it took her to take all my measurements and choose fabrics.

Thirty short minutes roll by as Janice and I talk about insignificant things. When the old lady comes out from the back, she says, "Come, try these on. I'll make adjustments." We follow her back through the velvet curtain, but this time there is a rack full of newly made outfits. *I think I counted around four different outfits, hanging on the rack.*

She hands me an outfit and points to the makeshift dressing room. By the time she finishes trying them all on and takes her notes, I'm even more exhausted than I was before. The outfits the lady made me wear are either black, brown, or neutral-colored.

The first is a warrior's outfit with a cloak and straps around my body, especially my waist, with places to hold my armory of knives, along with a pair of tall boots. The second is a traveler's attire, fitted with a cloak that has nearly fifty pockets on the inside, of all sizes. Some to fit coins, others to conceal a knife. The third is a light gray, loose-fitting affair with brown pants and a vest of sorts. Leather is sewn into the vest on its shoulders and around the collar. The last outfit is something I could wear to a ball: a sheer, black medieval shawl to go over my left shoulder and drape down by my waist. Underneath, there is a black button-up shirt and black slacks.

"Where am I going to wear these? Why do I need this many outfits?" I shoot my questions toward both Janice and the old lady.

"You never know when you will need a traveler's outfit, a warrior's outfit, or even when you will be expected to attend a formal event," the old lady says, gesturing toward a pile next to her. "This is a new backpack for you. The one you have won't work."

"Why not?" I love my backpack. *I remember Mom and I went school shopping this past fall. I never had a backpack I absolutely loved, but this one was perfect! It had many pockets and was a deep blue. It even had a spot for headphones. I love it!"*

The old lady shakes her head. "Everything you need now won't fit in your old one."

With that, she passes me my new backpack, which is more of a sack with drawstrings. I reluctantly take it as I carry both my bags over my shoulders. I collect my new wardrobe while Janice pays the lady, and we're off.

30

Small Elf Men Are Mean!

"Where are we going?" I ask Janice as we head toward a different direction than we came from before.

"We have to find a new way back," she responds.

"What? Why?" I ask, confused.

"The way we came only works for entering Lavina but not leaving. Plus, the door disappeared after we passed through it," she explains plainly.

We wander through the woods on a pale walking path for what seems like hours. I notice that Janice occasionally walks by tapping on the bark of a tree, listening then moving to the next one.

We abruptly stopp when we came across a tree that looked very different from the others. The tree is large and looks almost fake. Taking a few steps closer, I see why it's different. There's a faint line resembling an outline of a small door at the base of the trunk. Janice looks at me, putting a finger to her lips, indicating that I stay quiet, then glances back at the tree. I nod in response.

Janice knocks on the trunk, roughly where a doorknob

would be, similar to how she knocked on the others we passed. This time, something happens behind the bark, and the lines on the tree shift, forming a small door. Janice taps again just as a small creature pops its head out of a tiny sliding window I hadn't seen before. The small creature is the size of a restaurant to-go cup, with pointy ears and nose. His eyes are round and large, and he wears a green elf-like hat where his ears stick out to the sides. He looks between Janice and me as I hold my breath, keeping quiet. Janice lets out a large sigh as the small creature starts to shake his head. She reaches into her coat pocket and pulls out a coin on a chain. Handing him the chain- which is about his body length- his eyes widen three times their original size. He slams the window shut. I feel defeated, letting out the breath I still held. Janice stands there, tall and strong. The door carved into the tree trunk starts to open slowly.

"You ready?" Janice asks.

I nod, stunned by what's happening.

"NO!" the tiny creature squeaks in a high-pitched voice.

"What do you mean, no?" Janice challenges.

"Passage for you, not him," he responds.

"What? That chain and coin were worth more than two passages."

"NO!"

"Yes! Tell me why not."

"I don't know him. That's why!"

"He's new. No one knows him."

My gut starts doing flips and tightening.

"If no one knows him, how do I know he is worth it?"

"What? You never put me through this."

"I knew you."

"What can I do to prove I'm *worth it?*" I ask, not realizing I'm speaking.

"Hmm," the small elf man thinks. "I know!" He perks up. "I will give you two tests."

"Tests?" I ask nervously.

"Yes, first," he reaches behind him and pulls out a piece of paper covered in dirt and mud. "Here, I found this in the human world. Read it to me."

"What?"

"What's the point of this?" Janice asks.

"I need to see if he's worth it," the tiny creature says again. Taking the paper—larger than the little creature—my hands start to shake. My nerves are firing off, unsure of what I'm about to read. Skimming over the page, it's an old flyer for a movie. Based on the images, it's for the "Wizard of Oz" premiere. The graphics now have a dull pair of legs and shoes, faint red heels, and an extensive path—the Yellow Brick Road—in front of the shoes.

"Read!" the tiny creature shouts. Looking down at the paper, my hands begin to shake as I start to read.

"Th…e… Wizard…of…"

"No! Not the title. Everyone knows the title. Read the small printed stuff."

I really want to knock out this tiny creature and pass through the tree to get home. Glaring at the little elf, I try to focus on the words.

"Eye…n… Oh In… Thee…at…Theeatrs." My face flushes red. I can feel the heat rising, and my vision starts to blur.

"Keep going," the creature prods.

"In…Theeatres…" Deep breath. "In Theaters eve…re… where"

"Stop! Stop!" The creature exclaims.

Thank god. I take a deep breath.

"Give me that!" The tiny creature steps away from the door, then jumps up to my height and grabs hold of the paper on its way back down. "Now, the next test!"

"Did I pass the first one?" I ask.

"Here," he holds out a ticket book. I grab the book and look at its cover. It's similar to the flyer I was holding, but the words on it are different—shaped oddly.

"Read!" he shouts again.

Even though the words are shaped differently, I can read them, and it's exhilarating.

"In theaters everywhere for the first time in generations." *I want to continue reading, which is a first for me.*

"Yes! You are worthy!" the small man shouts, jumping up and down, again matching my height. He steps aside, allowing Janice and me to pass. Not wanting to second-guess what just happened, Janice and I exchange a quick nod and continue through the tree door. As we are walking down the dark, narrow tunnel in the tree, I ask Janice,

"What was up with those tests?"

"I think he planned to see if you were truly a Willorian."

"What does that mean?"

"Willorian's struggle with reading Earth English. Since you struggled, yet were able to read the words and even translate them back to English, you were deemed worthy."

"Interesting, but what was different about how the words were shaped?"

"Remember the words you drew in your sketchbook that resemble cross-hatching?"

"Yeah?" I say, confused.

"Willorian's alphabet derives from those symbols, mixed with the English alphabet. It's harder to learn,but since you already know and somewhat understand Earth English, it might have given you a general sense of the Willorian language. And how you understand the old symbols... well, that's beyond my comprehension."

We walk in silence for the remainder of the trip. The tunnel is cool, and when I run my fingers along the wall, some clay sticks to my palms. When we reach the end of the tunnel, Janice once again pulls out the device she had before, activating another door. *Hoping—no, praying—it leads to the abandoned building—my new home.*

When I open the door, no sun peeks around the edges. Instead, a dark cloud covers the sky, and I can see the moon, though it's shaded

"Let's get you to bed. You'll have a long day of practice tomorrow."

Nodding, feeling the sleep growing heavy on my eyelids, I make it up to my room. Not bothering to change or empty my new bag with my new wardrobe, I collapse onto the bed and immediately drift off.

31

Swordplay!

I wake up sometime later, unsure of the time. Pushing backthe curtains, I see the moon is still shining, but the sun is starting to rise

I notice movement in the distance. Squinting, I realize it's Echo practicing sword fighting. Unsure of what I should do, I lie there for a few more moments, allowing sleep to overtake me again. Sadly, sleep never came. Jumping out of bed, I decide to join Echo outside and hope she'll teach me some swordplay.

Grabbing hold of the drawstring bag filled with my new clothes, I dump everything out on my bed. Finding my new warrior outfit, I change and grab my sword, heading out to meet up with Echo. It will take some time to get used to these clothes. I'm not accustomed to having strips of leather wrapped around my waist. They make my body feel different.

Walking outside, the cold air hits my face, freezing everything. Thankfully, I don't feel it throughout the rest of my body—probably due to the new clothes.

"What did that tree ever do to you?" I ask Echo as I approach her. She is practicing her sword fighting movements against a very large tree trunk.

She stumbles backward. "You really shouldn't sneak up on someone who's wielding a sword."

"Yeah, but I figured you would have enough control not to slice me in half." I chuckle nervously.

"You think?" She looks at me at first, then a smirk spreads across her face, and she bursts into laughter. "So, what do you know about swordplay?" She asks.

"Um... I know how to swing it to kill black evil crows."

"Right! Well, you will need to learn a few more things than just swinging it at anything flying in front of your face."

"Probably. Yeah, that would be good."

"Here, let me show you."

Echo spends a considerable amount of time teaching me different methods: how to hold the sword, swing it, and block a swing coming toward me. I can feel my muscles tightening with each new movement. The sun is now rising fully, forcing the moon to retreat. As the air starts to warm, Echo speaks up.

"You've got this down pretty well, but you'll still need to practice. eep practicing against the tree. I'm going to shower and maybe catch some sleep before everyone else wakes up."

"Okay..." I say hesitantly. "Is it okay for me to be out by myself?"

"Of course! And hey, if anyone comes to attack you, you know how to fight them off." She smiles and laughs, grabs her things, and heads off. I wait until she enters the building before I resume practice. Normally, when people watch me, I get nervous, but with Echo helping me, I feel pretty comfortable.

Letting out a long, deep breath, I lift my sword, hitting the tree repeatedly. I continue until I hear a branch snap behind me. *I think Echo must have come back to practice or to watch. She must want to surprise me by testing my skills.*

I hear another branch snap, and leaves rustle a few feet behind me. She's closer now.

"Couldn't stay away, huh?" I say jokingly.

Lifting my arm, I turn to face her, but it's someone else. There's a dark-cloaked figure standing before me. I see it for a brief moment before another figure steps out into the clearing, holding a rock, moving faster than possible, and hitting me in the head. Everything goes black.

32

Darkness, My Old Friend.

Everything is dark. I can't see anything in front of me. Stretching out my hands, I realize I'm blindfolded. My fingers connect with something–or maybe it's someone–a body. One minute, I am trying to figure out where I am by feeling, then once again, I'm being hit in the head. Everything goes dark...again.

33

Knock Out!

When I come to this time, there is no blindfold. A severe headache pounds on my left temple, and I can't quite open my eyes all the way. I'm sore all over–my arms, ribs, and legs. Trying to look around, I see I'm at a makeshift camp. There's a fire blazing in a fire pit, but it will die out soon if no one adds more wood logs. A larger tent sits a few feet behind the fire pit, and I can make out the silhouette of at least one person inside, their movements barely visible. Pushing myself up, I bite my tongue to stifle a scream. Something feels broken. Defeated, I lay back down, resting my head on a soft patch of moss. Forcing myself to stay awake, I listen for any movement from the person inside the tent or any animals, hoping to determine where I am exactly.

A rustling sound comes from my left, and I freeze, closing my eyes and attempting to hold my breath. *If they think I am unconscious, they might spill some secrets or give away our location.* Whoever is moving closer taps my shoulder with the toe of their shoe, testing to see if I will react. I force my eyes shut tighter, suppressing the urge to scream as pain radiates from where I was hit. I exhale steadily as I hear them walk away, scuffing their feet against the leaves and sticks. I can hear them shuffling leaves and sticks away from something, as the heat of the fire rises, I hear tiny sparks hitting dry leaves around the fire pit.

I open my eyes slightly to see where the people are. The one who poked me is now in front of the tent, his head inside, blocking most of the opening with his body. Seizing the opportunity, I release the air I was holding and open my eyes fully, allowing them to adjust to the darkness. I shift slightly for comfort, unsure how long I have to stay like this. Hearing the tent flaps rustle, I freeze, listening.

"We need to find out what he knows," says a raspy voice.

"I know, I know, but he only knows stuff when he draws," replies a younger-sounding voice.

"Well, I'm sure he knows more than he's letting on. Let's wake him up!" says the raspy voice.

My body tenses. Closing my eyes once again, I hear two sets of footsteps approaching, noting the raspy-voiced person has a limp while the younger one moves lightly. I'm unprepared for their method of waking me up. A palm connects with my cheek, and I spring awake, eyes frantically scanning my surroundings. When my vision clears, I see two figures in full-body cloaks and face coverings, similar to the mystery figure who helped me in the woods and gave me my sword.

"Hey, kid!" The younger one shouts at me. "Wake up!"

I mumble, trying to get my throat and voice working.

"We need to know the future!"

"What?" I say groggily.

"Tell us what is going to happen," the raspy voice yells.

"It... it doesn't work that way. I can't just tell you. I don't even know what or how things happen." I spill out.

"See, I told you," as the younger one smacks the back of their hand against the raspy-voice figure's shoulder.

"Well, what do you need to see the future?" The raspy voice asks.

"My sketchbook," I wince, trying to sit up. "And my pencils, too."

"We will get you what you need," says the younger voice.

"How… how do you know about me?" I ask, sitting up.

"What?" They both say, caught off guard.

"How… how did you know I can see the future? Not many people know," I say again.

Before either of them can respond, the younger figure hits me against my head again, knocking me out once more.

34

Doomed!

I come to, watching the embers in the fire pit dance back and forth between the remnants of the logs. I must have been unconscious for a while since the log - the raspy-voiced figure placed it on the fire before I was knocked out - burned down again. *I'm going to continue to have severe headaches until I get out of here, especially if they continue to hit me in the head.*

Groaning slightly, I search for my captors without moving my body. I don't think I could move even if I tried.

"NO!" I hear a shout. "We don't need him! We will find the rest on our own," the raspy voice shouts. I can now make out that the voice belongs to the older male.

"Are you insane? Only he can tell us where the rest are. This map isn't helping at all," the younger voice retorts.

"Shh. Do you want to wake him?"

"Maybe we should. Maybe we can get him to tell us something else."

"I don't think knocking him out repeatedly is going to trigger his ability or give him a vision."

The younger figure doesn't say anything, only raises their arms in despair.

"Okay, okay," the younger voice concedes. "I'll stop knocking him unconscious. I promise."

I can tell they're discussing inside the tent, things I cannot hear.

"Okay, we know for sure there's a dragon scale in Lavina, but it's broken now. So something happened to it."

"Yes," the raspy male voice chimes in quickly. "But what about the others?"

"I know. I know. I'm trying to figure that out. Let's see. Wait, where did we check in, Eldridge?"

"The realm of Eldridge is full of spiders and venomous insects. I figured they would be in the center of their nest, but it wasn't there."

"Yeah, tell me about it. I'm still recovering," the younger voice hissed angrily. "Where else would it be?"

Before the older one can respond, the younger voice rushes out of the tent. "I've had enough!" he shouts.

He grips the front of my shirt, lifting me with ease. "Where are they? Tell me how to find them!"

Pain shoots out in every direction of my body. I can't help but scream in agony.

The raspy male comes running rather than limping out of the tent. "Put him down! Your short temper is going to get us into trouble. Let's give him the paper and pencils-maybe he will create something."

"Ugh, fine." He drops me back down to the ground with no concern for my welfare. I'm propped up against a tree trunk for support. I'm afraid my pain receptors are going to eventually overload from all the pain radiating through them.

"Here," the younger one grabs a bag near the fire pit and

throws it down at me. "Draw! Do what you do to see the future. We *need* to know what happens. And we need to know NOW!"

With that, they both turn around and walk away.

"He better produce something, and soon!"

35

Explosion?

Nothing appears on the page, even after I wake from dozing off. I'm running out of options. Maybe I could draw anything, hoping they'll take it as a vision—but what if it doesn't come true? What will happen to me then? I'm trapped here, in pain, forced to draw something, anything, just to see the future.

I haven't had anything to eat or drink since I've been here. My stomach growls loudly at the thought.

Moving my arm cautiously, I reach for the pencils and the pad of paper, letting muscle memory guide me despite my pain. My fingers curl around the pencil and brush the paper as my mind takes over. By the time my hand finally stills, I look down to see I have drawn nothing new, but there are things I see in front of me on the paper: the fire pit with the dying embers, the tent, the outline of the two figures, and the trees around me.

Movement off to my right catches my attention. I see one of the figures coming back, arms full of logs and grocery bags.

As he moves closer, he catches sight of me holding my pencils against the paper. He drops everything in a rush and runs over to me, snatching the paper from my hand.

"Did you? Wait... what's this?" He shouts, shaking the paper vigorously. He shakes the paper in front of my face. "This is nothing! Why did you draw these?" I have drawn the outlines of him and the younger one. His face contorts in anger as he tears the page into pieces and tosses it into the fire, reigniting the dying embers.

Well, there goes my memory of this place. Good riddance. I'm not sure I want to remember it anyhow.

"Draw...the...future! NOW!"

"I can't. I've told you it doesn't work like that!" I shout back, gripping my ribs.

He shouts and gestures, throwing his hands into the air. The man walks off limping, leaving the wood and the grocery bags where they fell.

--

Dozing off once again, it isn't until I hear more shouting that I wake up.

I can see the two figures arguing in the dim light inside the tent. I can barely hear their argument.

"What are you saying? He drew something, but you tore it up and tossed it into the fire."

"Yes, he doodled everything he saw in front of him: the fire pit, the tent, us!"

"So, what if it was part of a vision? And you didn't let him finish."

They go quiet. "Oh, I didn't think of that. Maybe he can redraw it."

"You never think!" the younger figure shouts as he walks over to the other side of the tent.

Looking down at the blank paper in front of me, I know I can redraw them, but should I? While I was pondering this, I was unprepared for what happened next.

A loud explosion erupts to the right of the tent, out in the distance. The trees around me shake, shedding their leaves and branches. I brace myself for the impact of branches hitting me, but I am thankful when it is only small twigs. The two figures from inside the tent rush out, looking in both directions, before bolting toward the explosion. Without looking back, they disappear into the darkness and trees.

Frantically looking in all directions, I try to lift my body off the ground but have no success. While they're gone, I have to get out of here. That's when I see it. Well, not *it*, but her! Echo is running toward me from the opposite side of the explosion. She's wearing, well, I'm not exactly sure what she is wearing. It looks like an all-black form-fitting dress with leather straps running up and down her body. She has a leather bag hooked to her waist. I can tell she has multiple knives sheathed along her ankles and arms. She has a charcoal hood shielding her face and hair, complete her ensemble. She... she looks amazing.

"Aidan... Aidan... are you okay?"

"What?" I ask, completely caught off guard.

"Are you hurt?"

"Yes... everywhere," I wince. "I think something is broken, too."

"Okay," she gestures to the woods, waving as a signal to others who may be hiding. A group of four exits the woods, all dressed in a similar fashion as Echo.

"Who?" I start.

"Shh, we'll get you back home and fix you."

Two people come near Echo, and I hear her giving them

directions on how to carry me.

"Wait," I say grabbing Echo's arm. "Check the tent," my voice is hoarse. "It sounded like they knew where some, if not all, of the dragon scales are. They knew Lavina had one, but it was broken. They also mentioned another realm. Oh, what was it? Oh! Eldrigge!"

She freezes and shudders. "Did you say Eldrigge?"

"Yes. Why?"

"Nothing to get into right now. We need to get you back and get our healer working on you."

The last thing I see before I drift off is Echo running into the tent and the two Unnaturals helping me onto a makeshift travois. Then, similar to last time, everything goes black. But this time, I'm not being knocked unconscious.

36

Screams!

There is a layer of fog ahead of me. I can't determine what is next to me because the fog is so thick. I edge forward, praying I don't run into anything. Everything is hazy. Closing my eyes, I try to focus my thoughts. The fog slowly begins to subside, as if a wind is pushing it out of the way. As the fog dissipates, a building emerges from the mist. I try to make out what it is until it hits me–literally. I quickly duck as if something is being shot out from the building. Crouching and breathing heavily, I feel my body running toward the house, not away, as it should. I push through the fog and dodge the objects flying from the building.

When I come to a stop, kneeling and looking around me, I see I am not in front of any building but the Mystery House. But something's different. I am between the house and its iron gate. I don't remember entering the gate, only avoiding what was flying from the house. Catching my breath again, I look up to see the house is… moving. It's only a tiny adjustment, but it is moving. Then I hear it before I see it. The front door starts to creak open, similar to a horror movie when the front door creaks open before someone or something jumps out and scares the viewer.

The door grinds open, but before I can make out what lies behind it, a beeping sound causes me to stop. Looking around, I can't find where the sound is coming from. Then I'm being pulled–no, dragged along the ground. Back through the iron gate and down the street. I wake in a bed with white curtains hanging around it. Attempting to move my arm, I realize I'm soaked in sweat.

"What?" I frantically look around, out of breath.

"Whoa, calm down," someone next to me says. I can't distinguish who shouted as everything in my vision is fuzzy. I can't… I can't see. Or I can't distinguish figures.

"What's happening?" I shout louder than I intend.

"Calm down, kid," the mystery voice says. "Hey, can we get some extra help over here?"

"No! No! They will get me. They're going to force me to draw. No! I can't!" I'm screaming and kicking anything that comes my way.

Three large Creatures are running toward me. *Can that be? No, it can't be. Do they have tails?* From what I can tell, the people–or Unnaturals, or maybe Creatures, hopefully, good creatures–have long tails. They make it over to my bed and start running their hands over my head and body. Their hands are glowing. Before I can scream out again, my eyes get heavy, and everything goes dark.

When I wake again, I've been strapped down to the bed, but I have no recollection of what happened or why. When I look to my right, I see Echo asleep. She is sitting in an oversized chair, and I try not to watch her sleep, not wanting to be creepy, but she seems to be at peace. No worries, no fears, nothing. Just peaceful.

I try to stretch, but I'm unable to due to the bindings. When I move my arms, the bindings rattle against the metal bed railings, causing Echo to stir.

"Sorry," I whisper. "Didn't mean to wake you. I'm trying to stretch but seem to be stuck."

"You're all good," she replies quietly.

"Why... why am I bound to the bed?" I ask, still in shock at my condition.

"You woke up a while ago, and you were thrashing and screaming. The meds fear you might try to hurt yourself or others. When they come to do the check-up, they'll probably release you from the bindings," she says, looking hopeful.

"Okay!"

"How are you feeling?"

"Fine. Sore. Did I break something?"

"Yeah, you were covered in bruises and a sprained ankle. Thankfully, it wasn't a full break."

"Oh, okay... that's good."

"How did you know where I was? How did you find me?"

We see movement by the door of the room.

"We can talk about that when you're better and out of here," she whispers. "But don't worry, we got the scale and the map."

"What?"

Before she say me more, she ducks out of sight, hiding under a different cloth-covered bed. *Is she not supposed to be here? I wonder. If so, then why? If she was the one to find me and bring me back, why can't she visit me?*

37

The Truth?

Five days later, I'm released from the medical ward. It feels great to get out and finally be able to walk on my own. Echo helps me out of there and leads me back to the room I stayed in before all this happened. I smile and feel warm in my stomach when I see all my things still where I left them. My sword lies on my desk, and there seems to be a present on the end of my bed.

Hobbling over to my bed, I sit beside the wrapped box and reach for it. Grabbing hold of its shape, it feels heavy, similar to a stack of textbooks. *Please don't tell me I have to learn History or English after being released from a prison where I wasn't allowed to do anything. Five days of being inhibited, unable to do a single thing.* Their orders stated I needed to "heal my mind and body."

Echo sits down at the desk in front of me. I pull the ribbon off, letting it fall to the ground, and curl back up once it makes contact. Peeling back the paper, I see it's not a stack of History or English books, but two heavy-duty hardcover sketchbooks and one paperback sketchbook. There's a new set of sketch pencils, too!

Gasping "Wow! This is amazing! Who are these from?"

"Was there no card?" Echo asks.

Looking toward her, I can tell she is trying to hide a sheepish smile.

"Are they from you?"

She only shrugs in response.

"Come on, tell me! Are they?"

"Fine, they're from Janice and me." she caves, "We got them for you when you were recovering, but they wouldn't let us give them to you because you needed to *rest*. Which, by the way, I thought was stupid too."

"Thank you!" I stammer out. "This is the best gift ever!"

"Well, you're welcome." She smiles.

"Hey, when I was in the infirmary, you told me you would tell me how you found me."

"Right!" She says, sounding as though I caught her off guard.

I grab one of the new sketchbooks, open it up, and grab a pencil.

She comes over and takes a seat next to me on the bed. Taking a deep breath, she lets it out slowly and begins, "After I returned to my room to shower and sleep a bit more, I was surprised I didn't see you for the rest of the morning. I checked both places, thinking you were still practicing or sleeping the day away. I checked your room first, then when you weren't there, I went to where I left you outside. That's when I saw it. I saw your sword lying on the ground, and I could tell some kind of fight had occurred by looking at the scuff marks on the ground. I followed what looked like drag marks until I lost the trail. I headed back to inform Janice what had happened and that we needed to rescue you. We formed a group to help rescue you and create a distraction. We brought on two Unnaturals who love making explosions and who made the distraction. Then, we brought the two Unnaturals, who are medically trained to carry you out if needed, which I'm glad we did. Then, I recruited a tracker. Trackers work like bloodhounds on Earth, though they are Unnaturals, not dogs." She chuckles. "He was able to track where they took you. When we found where you were, I had the two Unnaturals work on a distraction to get your captors away from you and brought in the medical team."

"I'm glad you found me. I was nervous about what would happen if no one did. They were forceful in trying to get me to use my powers."

"Really? Oh, that reminds me. Before the Unnatural medics took you away, you told me to run into the tent to grab their papers."

"Yeah! I remember. Did you find anything?"

"Yes, and I know where we have to go. You mentioned something about Eldrigge, and their map confirmed the location. They had one dragon scale, which they broke in half and drained of its magic."

"Map?"

"Yes, they have a map of all the realms. Some had lines crossed through them, and some didn't. Some have one asterisk, while others have three asterisks. There was no legend on what the lines and asterisks mean, but I assume the lines through the realm indicade there was no scale there, and the asterisks may suggest they had a strong belief that something could be there. Even though we don't know what this all means, we do know something."

"What's that?" I ask, putting my sketchbook aside and sitting up straighter.

"The people who took you are the ones who are trying to find all of the dragon scales and wrote the note that was sent to you. They're the ones who want to *balance the world and magic once more*!"

38

Legend?

Who knows what could have happened if Echo didn't find me? What would they have done if I couldn't produce any drawings or drawings they believed were visions? Taking a deep breath, I look at the stack of sketchbooks Echo and Janice had gifted me. While Echo was explaining what happened and how she found me, I was doodling mindlessly. Now, looking at the image I had doodled, I don't recognize it at first—but then it hits me. I had a vision while I was awake! The only way I can determine it's a vision is because of the symbols at the bottom of the page. *I have since learned that doodles don't have symbols at the end; only visions do.*

I close my book and quickly run out of my room with my sketchbook. As I race down the hallways, I look in every room, searching for Echo. I'm about to take a sharp right when I nearly collide with the small elf boy who helped me earlier. Stopping short, I realize there's now a second version of him standing behind me, smiling. *Weird. How?* Then I realized I didn't run into him–he has super speed. He gives me a quick wink and then zooms off, leaving a cloud of dust behind him.

Shaking my head in disbelief, I continue my search for Echo.

I reach the end of the hallway when I hear her voice talking to someone I don't recognize. Creeping forward silently, I listen.

"What do you mean Calix is missing?" Echo whispers harshly.

"He...he has been gone for a while now, but I figured he was sulking and on his own mission," says the mystery voice.

"But he isn't allowed to go out on his own. He knows better; he doesn't have his powers anymore," Echo shrieks.

Calix doesn't have his powers? Realization dawns on me–that's why he got so upset when I was pushing to know his power. He doesn't have them anymore. I feel so stupid now.

Echo takes a long, deep breath in and out. Even without seeing her, I can tell she is either rolling her eyes or pressing her fingers to her eyelids and rubbing them. I've noticed she often does this when she's stressed.

"Do we have any clue where he went?"

"No, although I haven't checked his room yet."

"Give me his key. I will go check it out."

I hear keys jingle, and then I hear movement, but it's too late. Echo comes around the corner, stopping short.

"How much did you hear of that conversation?" she asks.

"All of it," I say sheepishly.

"Ugh," she rolls her eyes. "Want to come with?"

"Where?"

"To check his room."

"Sure."

We walk up to the third floor and halfway down the hallway. Upon reaching his room, I notice Echo is extremely tense.

"Do you know what to expect?"

"N-No," was all she stammered.

"Would you like me to go first? I know you're close friends with him."

She shakes her head. "Apparently, I'm not as close with him as I thought. I didn't even know he was gone or MIA." She lets out an exaggerated breath then pushes the key into the keyhole. With a turn, she pushes the doorknob down and opens the door, letting it swing open. We both freeze, gasping at the sight before us.

His walls are covered from floor to ceiling with newspapers and sticky notes. *The chaotic display reminds me of an old serial killer documentary my mom used to watch.* His desk is cluttered, with a lamp still on, but the light is dimming—I can tell it's been on since he left. Echo turns to one side of the room, and I go to the other. We take it all in, silently absorbing the scene. I notice newspapers tacked to the wall with headlines covering strange events in different realms; there's even a newspaper from Earth. How is that even possible?

"Aidan, come over here," Echo urges.

"What did you find?"

"This," she says, passing me a map similar to the one she found in my captors' tent.

"How many maps are there?" I ask.

"I don't know, but I wonder if they have a map of all the realms, marked with the same slashes and asterisks as our other map. This one, however, has a legend off to the side:

```
/ = no scales
*= possibility of a scale sighting
**= actual sighting
***= need to look here asap.
```

LEGEND?

```
$ = buyers
$$ = original buyer↺
 = relook➶
 = protectors of realm (prep)⤊
 = house sighting
```

My heart drops when I see the last one— "house sightings." Does this mean he's close to finding the source of all magic? Could he be the younger voice I heard from my captors? I try to think back to my last conversation with Calix and the voice I heard during my kidnapping. Could it really be him?

"There's a legend," Echo exclaims. "Great, we can compare these two maps with the legend."

"Yeah," I say, half paying attention.

"You okay?"

"Yeah, I think so. No, no, I'm not. Ugh, I don't want to tell you this because you are friends with him, but," I take a shuddering breath, "I think he was one of my kidnappers."

"What?" She's shocked, turning toward me.

"I think. I didn't see his face, but his voice was very similar to the one I heard.

She frantically shakes her head back and forth, not believing what I'm saying.

She shies away from me, avoiding my gaze as if she can't bear to look at me right now. When I turn back to the wall, something catches my eye. Grabbing my sketchbook, I notice the striking similarity—it's uncanny. What I drew earlier matches one of the maps on the wall.

"Echo? I think I know where we have to go."

"What?" She turns back, her eyes welling up in tears.

I hold up my sketchbook, aligning the page of my new drawing with the map on the wall.

"What?" Her voice trembles now.

"We have to go here." I point to both drawings.

"Ohixar."

39

Call Home!

"Absolutely not! Neither of you nor anyone else is traveling there!" Janice shouts at us.

"But that's the best place to find the next dragon scale—and maybe Calix."

Absolutely NOT!" she repeats, her voice rising.

"We're going," Echo says sternly, her gaze unwavering. "You can either come or stay, but we're leaving."

After a tense standoff, Janice reluctantly relents. "Fine, but you'll be taking the best warriors we have. I have a feeling there will be a fight waiting for your arrival."

"Deal!" Echo replies, grinning widely.

—

Echo and I have been packing for the last hour. I've stuffed my meager belongings into my school backpack, its zippers straining to hold everything in.

"Didn't the seamstress give you a drawstring bag?" Echo asks.

"Yes, why?"

"Use that. You'll have plenty of room."

I eye her suspiciously, unsure if she has seen the bag. It's smaller than my backpack, but as I transfer my belongings into the drawstring bag, I realize there's more than enough room. *To be honest, this bag reminds me of Mary Poppins' carpet bag—endlessly spacious.* I chuckle but feel a pang of sadness when I remember how Mom used to watch the movie after Dad would come home for a short time and then leave again.

"Hey, is there a way I can send a message or call my Mom before we head to this new realm?"

"Sure! We can do it after we finish packing, right before leaving."

"Great!"

We complete our packing, and to my surprise, everything fits into the drawstring bag. Echo leads me to a small, dimly lit room I hadn't noticed before.

"Okay, here we are," she says, pointing to a table full of herbs and candles.

"What is this?"

"There are two ways to contact someone from here to another realm. I figured you'd prefer to talk with her sooner rather than later. The first option is sending the message in an envelope and waiting for someone to pass through a Nexus to Earth to be mailed through snail mail. The second option is a bit more complicated but more effective—magic!"

"Do you mean magic, magic? Like a spell?"

"Yes! We normally don't dabble in spell magic, but this is the best method we have found for communication between realms."

"Why didn't Janice tell me about this option?"

"She's not a big fan of using spell magic unless necessary.

"Okay..." I say, feeling uneasy.

"It's fine. Let's start. All you have to do is write your Mom's full—first, middle, and last— on this bay leaf with a marker. This will ensure it reaches the right person. Then I'll leave the room. You'll light the candle, whisper her name and reason for the call, and it will connect to her. If she doesn't pick up, it will act like a voicemail, but instead, on her phone, it will send an impression of your message in her mind. Does that make sense?"

"No, but let's do it," I say, trying to sound hopeful.

"Okay! I like this new attitude," Echo says, preparing the materials. "Here's the marker and the bay leaf. Write her full name. I'll step out now, and when you're done, blow out the candle and come out."

I nod, and Echo leaves. I light the candle and whisper her name, repeating, "Call Mom, call Mom, call Mom." The room echoes with a sound mimicking a ringtone. Then I hear her. Her voice, "Hello? Who's this?" She spits out.

"Mom?" I say, struggling to hold back my tears.

"Aidan? Is that you?" I can hear her voice breaking.

"Yes!" Tears stream down my cheeks.

"Oh, honey, how are you? Where are you? Are you in Willorian?"

"I'm great. I miss you. Yes, I'm in Willorian. I wanted to let you know I'm okay and hope to be home soon."

"When?" she practically shouts, now crying.

"I don't know exactly, but soon. I'm going on a mission to help save this world, Willorian. Once it's over, I'll come home!"

"Oh, honey, please come home soon. I'm sorry," she says, crying. Then I hear voices in the background, and she clears her throat. "Oh, honey, I have to go. They need me back. I love you, honey."

"I love you too, Mom. I'll be home soon. I promise."

With a gentle wisp of my breath, I lean forward and blow out the flickering candle. The candle extinguishes itself, only leaving a wisp of smoke curling into the air.

40

Adventure?

Echo, the two Unnatural warriors —Zia and Bren—join me as we head out, meeting in the center square. Echo transports each of us separately to Ohixar. Thankfully, Ohixar is in the same vicinity as the Willorian realms, so we plan on taking a Nexus.

Upon arrival in Ohixar, I notice we were all dressed in warrior outfits. Echo is wearing the same outfit she had on when she rescued me from the kidnappers. Zia's outfit is similar, though it has fewer knife pockets, and Bren's attire resembles mine. We are all prepared for a fight if one arises.

The landscape of Ohixar unfolds before us: mountains with exaggerated, pointed peaks and oddly-shaped structures forming arches in the distance. Enormous trees, towering as tall as skyscrapers and as wide as a city block, dominate the scenery. Nestled between two massive trees is a small town. The sky and air around us are shrouded in a dark, gloomy blue, hinting at a possible lack of sunlight here.

"Has anyone been here before?" I ask the group.

"No," they reply in unison.

Before us stands a single path lined with bushes until it drops into an endless cliff, "Okay… let's take the path, and remember—no one falls," I say, trying to sound authoritative.

They all nod, and we start walking.

We have been walking for what feels like an hour or more. The path offers little interest, transitioning sporadically from grass to dirt to small rocks and back to grass. It's clear not many people travel this route. The path is wide enough for us to walk two by two, but we must be cautious of the steep drop-off on either side.

We all abruptly halt when we come to a fork in the road.

"Which way do we go now?" Echo asks.

"Um… I'm not quite sure," I reply.

"It's hard to tell which direction we need to go since the city still looks like it's in front of us. But if we go one path, it could lead us away from the city," Zia notes.

"Is there a specific reason we're attempting to walk toward the city?" Bren asks, clearly confused.

"Most likely, the dragon scale would be in the city, where someone or somewhere can protect it," Echo explains.

"But no one is supposed to know where the dragon scale is? It's designed to protect itself from Unnaturals and Creatures discovering it," Bren counters.

"Yes, but if someone had the ability to see it or know if the dragon scale still holds its power, it would likely be in a bright and powerful place," Echo responds.

"Or maybe not," I interject.

"What do you mean?" Echo asks.

While they were talking, I started looking around. "Are we sure the scale is giving off bright and powerful magic?"

"Based on the amount of asterisks on the map–yes," Echo

responds.

"Okay..." I muse, surveying the sky and the spare vegetation. An idea begins to form. "What if—and hear me out—what if the power here is not bright and powerful but dull and weak?"

"It's a possibility," Echo admits.

Observing the dark sky and then the path, I notice that one to the right is bright and lush, while the one to the left is barren, with a dead bird lying a few feet from us.

"Your point?" Zia interrupts.

"What are the common signs of a Ripple?" I ask the group.

Echo's eyes light up. One by one, she begins to tick off each sign on her fingers. As her fist closed, I watch as her index and middle fingers flicks past her thumb, extending outward, followed by her thumb trailing behind. Counting off each one, "Dead plants, dead animals, or possibly strange animals. Low power is usually farther away from the Ripple, while stronger power is closer."

"Exactly! What if it's the same for the scales?"

"It's worth a try," Echo says, bouncing excitedly.

"Great! To the left we go," I announce, looking over at Zia and Bren, who shrug and follow us down the path.

"But if this isn't the way, we'll try the other path," Zia says nonchalantly.

41

Tree Of Life?

As time passes, we walk along the path, and the sky retains its dark blue hue. I can't help but wonder how the people here tell time when the sky doesn't change.

"Do we know how much further?" Bren asks.

I stay quiet because I have no idea.

"No," Echo responds curtly.

We continue walking along the desolate path.

As time slips by unnoticed, I keep my mind occupied by counting every sixty seconds, then steps per second, per minute, and stride. After twenty minutes, I abandon my mental counting. Glancing from the ground to the sky, I see a large tree looming ahead, reminiscent of Disney's Tree of Life. Its bark is rough and deeply ridged, with the trunk fanning out like large fingers anchoring themselves into the ground. Scanning its massive trunk, I see thick branches extending in every direction, each limb as thick as a car. The tree's crown—where the branches and leaves meet—seems to stretch a mile into the sky. I can barely make out the different shades of green. Vines swing down from some of the large branches, evoking images of a jungle. A makeshift rope bridge sways in the wind, catching my attention as it connects one large branch to another on a distant tree.

"This tree would make a cool tree fort," Zia says.

"Let's take a break and climb up to check it out. I bet the view is amazing!" Bren exclaims, stopping and taking off his pack.

"No!" Echo snaps. "We need to keep going."

"Come on, Echo. We have been walking for hours. We can take a five or even ten-minute break," Zia argues, siding with Bren.

Before Echo can object further, Bren and Zia have already dumped their packs and swords on the ground. They take a few steps back, running and jumping to grab the vines swinging from the branches. Using their momentum, they swiftly ascend the tree trunk.

"Where was that energy an hour ago?" Echo mutters under her breath.

"I'm not sure, but I wish I could borrow some of their energy and excitement," I remark.

"I guess we have no choice. Let's take a break," Echo says with a shrug.

"I guess," I reply, trying to hide a smile. My feet have been aching for most of our walk, but I didn't want to complain and make everyone stop just because of my aching feet.

Echo and I both drop our sacks and sit down on the ground. Echo pulls her pack closer, taking out a snack bar and a water bottle.

She gestures, offering me a bar, and I take it, grateful that she was clever enough to pack them—something I had forgotten.

We sit there, relaxing while I rub my ankles and attempt

to stretch them without taking off my shoes. We sit there in silence, too quiet.

"Do you hear them?" I ask Echo.

"No, I don't," she replies, sounding worried.

"Hey, guys, you good?" I shout up into the trees.

Silence. Only the wind rustling the leaves answers us.

"Guys?" Echo shouts again.

Still nothing.

Panic surges through me, and I see Echo is also starting to panic.

"Maybe the tree is too high for them to hear us," I suggest hopefully, though I don't fully believe it.

"Maybe," Echo says, starting to rummage through her bag. "But I don't have a good feeling about this."

"What are you looking for?" I ask just before she pulls out what looks like a Willorian emergency kit.

It has the same logo—a red cross on top of the container—similar to the ones back home, but when she unzips it, items spill out. A fire stick, bandages, full-size water bottles, a can of bug spray, protein snacks, even some sugar treats, and a miniature flashlight. Then some unusual things start appearing: rope, brass knuckles, not one but two swords matching the size of mine, and multiple throwing knives. Echo dumps everything out of the bag, spreading its contents on the ground. She grabs the rope, one of the swords, and a few of the throwing knives.

As she hastily stands, she tells me to grab what I can. Unsure what to choose, I pick up the brass knuckles, the sugar treats, the flare, bug spray, and two extra throwing knives.

Echo looks at me, puzzled. "That's an odd mix of stuff you picked."

"I wasn't sure what to grab, so I took anything close by."

"Fair enough." She shrugs. "Okay, hold onto me." She transports us to the top of the tree.

As we regain our balance and look around, we don't see Zia or Bren until we hear them.

"HELP!" they scream, but from where?

"Help us!" The cry fades as if they are being carried or taken away. Echo and I start frantically searching —looking down at the path we came from, among the other trees—without success.

After several minutes of searching, Echo shouts. "There!" She frantically points towards the bridge separating the two trees. Zia and Bren are struggling, on the verge of being whisked away. Their hands are bound, and while their mouths are partially covered, Zia has managed to get her gag off and is screaming for help.

"Help!" Zia cries again just before the kidnapper strikes her in the head, causing her to go limp. Bren falls forward when Zia goes down. I hadn't realized that there was a rope binding their wrists together.

"We need to get over there and help them," I tell Echo firmly.

"Yes, grab hold!" Echo shouts. I do, and Echo transports us onto the bridge.

"Let them go!" she shouts as we land on the rickety bridge.

I tentatively step forward, but Echo shoots her hand out to stop me.

"Look," she says, pointing toward the captives. "Isn't that...?"

"It is!" The captors are the same cloaked figures who attacked and kidnapped me. This time, they have Zia and Bren.

"Echo!" I shout over Bren's anguished cries for Zia. *Knowing there's something special between them that hasn't been shared with the rest of the group yet. Bren always follows Zia as if she is the leader, which makes me think that they like each other or that Bren really likes her.* "Can you get them out of here?" I continue to ask.

"I can try, but it'll have to be one at a time," she shouts back.

"Okay, get me over to the other side of the bridge, closest to the smaller figure. I'll try to distract the cloaked figures while you cut Zia and Bren's ropes and get them out of here."

"Okay," she says, trying to sound confident, though I can see she's nervous. Before I have a chance to take a deep breath, she grabs my arm and moves us to the other side of the bridge.

"Hey!" I shout, waving my hands and swords. "Come and get me!"

The smaller-sized figure comes charging toward me, shaking the bridge forcefully. I glance up to see where Echo is and notice she's still struggling to separate Zia and Bren's ropes.

Come on, Echo. Hurry up. I wish I had a way to communicate with her without drawing attention to her. I'm not sure where the other figure went. Only the younger, more petite figure is in front of me. He draws his blade just as I hear Zia wake and scream out in pain. The smaller-sized figure sharply turns around to see Echo transport Zia to the ground, leaving Bren behind. The younger figure changes course abruptly and heads toward Bren, who stumbles to regain his balance. He isn't fast enough and won't have enough time to draw his sword.

I reach for the items I had brought, and a chemistry class idea springs to mind: the bug spray and the flare. The younger figure draws back his wielded arm just as I snap the flare, igniting its fiery red and orange blaze, and toss it into the air. I rush my steps backward. As the flare begins to descend, I spray the canister. The chemicals mix with them, creating a roaring fire that propels itself toward the younger figure with the sword. But I'm too late.

Everything is moving in slow motion. By the time the fire is raging in front of me, I see the younger figure's sword pierce Bren's chest, slicing through his body with a deathly stroke. The fire catches on the young figure's cloak and engulfs Bren. I can only hope he dies quickly–not having to endure both the blade and fire I started.

The screams are all I can hear next. Zia's agonized wails pierce the air from the ground below. In that split second, between her cries and the fire still blazing, I realize that the bridge has also caught fire and is beginning to burn away.

1. A moment later, all I can hear is the rush of wind as the bridge collapses.

Illustration drawn by Tina Bartlett

42

I...Can't...Breathe...

The wind rushes past my face as I plummet toward the ground, fear gripping me. There's no net or anything to break my fall, only the certainty of a deadly impact. But then I see her... a familiar figure—Janice. She's here, her hands raised and chanting something.

Her shouting blends with the howling wind, or maybe it's just that I'm so close to the ground, and everything feels terrifyingly close. The ground rushes closer and closer. I shut my eyes tightly, bracing for the impact, expecting either sudden death or the excruciating pain of every bone in my body breaking.

I start counting, trying to gauge how close the ground is—five... four... three... two... two... two... nothing. I should have hit the ground by now—or maybe I did, and I'm dead. Is this heaven? I slowly open my eyes to see I'm floating a foot and five inches above the hard ground. Looking around, I see the figure who was on the bridge with me floating mid-air next to me. The fire scorched his robe, but it still covered his face.

"Watch out!" Janice shrieks, a second too late. I glance back and see her releasing her power just before we crash into the hard ground.

"Ow!" I murmur into the dirt. But I don't stay down for long.

"Duck!" Janice shouts at Echo as a blade hurtles toward her head. I quickly grab one of the small throwing knives from my hip, my sword ready in my right hand, preparing for what's about to unfold.

Echo stands, pulling a blade from the layers of leather she's wearing, and tries to strike at the taller figure.

"Why?" the taller figure asks in his raspy tone.

"Why? What?" Echo demands, slicing through the air with each word.

"Why him?" he asks, pointing his sword at me.

Echo looks briefly confused, then seizes the opportunity he's given her. She slashes at his arm, resulting in him dropping his sword. He swiftly grabs her other long sword. The raspy-voiced man clutches his injured arm. Though I can't see his eyes, his rigid posture and furious demeanor show how enraged he is. I yell toward Echo, "ECHO, GET DOWN!" But she doesn't hear me in time. The raspy-voiced man unleashes a power surge that sends her flying into the air, dropping her knives and swords and hurtling her toward the path's edge and over the ravine.

A gut-wrenching feeling twists in my stomach. She... she's gone...The thought consumes me as I grip my swords tighter, ready to fight. I'm jolted from my focus when the younger figure before me speaks.

"It was only a matter of time before she got herself killed."

"What?" I choke out, struggling to hold back tears and a

scream.

"She was always putting herself in unnecessary danger." The voice draws nearer.

I can't see him clearly; All I see is a blinding RED RAGE!

Suddenly, he's right in front of me. "What did you say?" I spit out again, my voice trembling.

"She... had... it... coming..." he repeats, and this time, he pulls off the remainder of his hood, revealing his face.

I was right. It's Calix.

43

The Fight!

The cloaked figure I suspected to be Calix was indeed him. But why? Why was he trying to kill me? Why did he team up with the raspy-voiced figure, and where was that figure now? A thousand questions flash through my mind at breathtaking speed.

I've already lost Echo. I *don't have time to dwell on her just yet.* I'm not about to lose Janice or Zia. Bren, we'll collect and spread his ashes if Zia chooses. Maybe Janice can retrieve Echo's body from the ravine, and we can do the same. My heart aches for all the deaths today.

"Hello, Aidan," Calix says, stretching out each word.

"Why?" I ask, my voice strained.

"Why what?" he chuckles.

"Why turn your back on Willorian? Why betray Echo? Why are you attacking me?"

"That's a lot of 'why' questions," he sneers. "How about instead, we fight, and if you *happen* to win, I'll tell you. Or, by the time you've finished thinking of all of your "why" questions, I might have already won this battle." He burst into laughter.

Not seeing any other options, I move my body into a stance Echo taught me.

"Fine," I spit out, grinding my teeth together.

"Good!" Before I have a chance to react, he swings around, slicing my arm with his sword.

I shriek in pain.

Janice starts to step forward, but I give her a sharp look and shake my head. She can't intervene. I can't afford to lose another friend today.

Grunting, I swing my sword, narrowly missing his head. "Where is your companion?" I demand, noticing he has vanished.

"Don't know, don't care," he replies, spitting out each word as he swings at me.

I dodge his swing, and he overextends, allowing me to knock him down. He crumples to the ground as the back of my sword hits him in the shoulder blades.

"Remember last time you beat me up?" I spit out. "Well, today, that changes."

"Oh, yes, how are your injuries?" he asks with mock concern.

"I healed."

"Good. It wouldn't be fair for me to fight you if you were still injured, although you sprained your ankle a week ago. That must still hurt," he says, pouting his lower lip. *I know he's trying to get under my skin, and it's working, but I refuse to give him the satisfaction.*

"Yeah, I think you or your friend had something to do with that. Was it you or him who kicked my ribs?"

"Oh, that was me. Purely for my enjoyment," he says with a devilish smile.

"Figures."

We fight intermittently. Just as I think I have him and victory is within reach, a sound catches me entirely off guard.

"Aidan," a soft-spoken voice calls out over the ravine.

No, it can't be. She went completely over the precipice. She was lost, gone.

"Aidan!" the soft voice pleas again.

"Oh, is your girlfriend calling you? You better save her," Calix taunts with a snake-like hiss.

How can I fight him and save her at the same time?

"Janice!" I shouted. "Get them out of here!"

Calix shoots a glare at her, momentarily forgetting she was there. "No!" he roars, starting to throw daggers with his unarmed hand—a mistake I should have noticed. Janice takes the opportunity to grab Zia's unconscious body and disappears. The look she gives me before she vanishes is full of apology. I nod in acknowledgment before she blinks out of sight.

"Now you're all alone with your girlfriend hanging by a thread, and you might not have much more to give," Calix sneers. "Oh, I almost forgot the main reason you guys ventured here— you were looking for this." Instead of the daggers, he pulls out a gleaming dragon scale, intact and not split in half.

"Okay," I say calmly, trying to match his nonchalant tone. "Just hand over the scale, and we'll call it even."

"Hmm, I think not," he replies.

I hear movement behind me and pray it's Echo attempting to pull herself out of the ravine. It's not. Instead, my whole body freezes as I see everything in slow motion, *like an active premonition.* I observe everything unfolding and choose to act on it—a way for all of us to make it out of this alive.

Calix tosses the dragon scale high into the air in slow motion as a gut-wrenching feeling settles in my stomach as if someone is watching me from behind. Ignoring the unsettling sensation, I seize the opportunity while he looks up and drives my sword deep into his chest. The impact of metal connecting with bone sends a shiver through me. His expression shifts from confidence to absolute fear, and his face falls flat. He collapses to the hard ground as the scale begins its descent. I see Echo climbing up the ravine, a rope dangling over the edge—likely secured and tossed to her by Janice before her departure. Echo manages to reach solid ground, struggling to maintain her balance.

The scale is now within reach. Despite my lack of athletic abilities, I hope to catch it. I leap, praying my timing is right to snatch the scale from the air and land safely. Jumping, I grasp the scale midair but fear the landing. Holding my breath, I see Echo near the ravine, and then she's gone. I don't see her again until I hit the ground, clutching the dragon scale tightly in my arms.

"Get off me," a voice shouts from beneath me.

"What?" I ask, quickly moving. It's Echo— she used her body to buffer my fall. Whether she did it to protect me or the scale doesn't matter. We both stand, examining the dragon scale, when we hear a gurgling noise behind us.

"Ha, you think you're so clever for finding the dragon scale. There are still sixteen more scales out there, and we weren't the only ones searching for them."

"What do you mean? Tell me what you know!" I shout at Calix, who now has blood forming in his mouth from his wound.

He doesn't get a chance to say another word as a smile rests on his face when he lets out his last breath.

"Great!" Echo says sarcastically. "So there are others out

there trying to find the dragon scales. For what, is it magic?" Echo states plainly.

"Yup! Seems that way," I remark.

"Great..." She grabs the bags we had earlier dumped on the ground, dusting them off. Looking over, Echo sees Bren's body, covered in burns and black char.

"We should burn his body and take his ashes home for Zia. They were the only family either of them had," Echo says sadly.

"I was thinking the same thing," I tell her with a forced smile.

—

We return home to Willorian with Bren's ashes and give them to Zia. It turns out her power was to shapeshift. We found her mid-transforming into a wolf, and when we handed her Bren's ashes, she took gingerly between her teeth and ran off.

We give the new dragon scale to Janice, who said she had a secure place for these highly magical items that need their own protection.

After things calmed down, I called Mom to let her know I would be home later that night. I still have a few more things I need to wrap up here. I'm tagging along with some other Unnaturals who are searching for someone to create a Nexus that will take us all home.

Echo and I discussed a game plan for when I would return, especially if I can find a Ripple. Little does she know I have a link with *the house* and a possible direct way back. *I still don't feel comfortable telling anyone, even Echo, who I've grown close to in the last few days.* Janice made it clear we have to find the other dragon scales before the others, *whoever they were,* find them first. Especially before they find and break the scales in half, taking the power for themselves. Echo and I agreed we would meet again in a month and message weekly or as often as possible. I pack my mediocre items in my sack and begin for home.

Just before I set out to leave, Janice catches up with me.

"Hey, great job today, well, every day since you've come to Willorian. I heard everything you saw and experienced. It's definitely different from a typical day here, but you did amazingly well. Thank you for sending a distress signal; if you hadn't, I fear I would have had to bring more than one body home. When are you planning on coming back?"

What distress signal? I didn't do anything that I can recall.

Shaking my head, making a mental note to bring that up later. "I told Echo I'd try to check back in a month. I will also search for any signs of a Ripple on Earth now that we know what to look for." I chuckle. "We devised a plan to start searching for the other dragon scales and use the map we found in Calix's tent. We think that will help lead us in the right direction."

"Good idea. Well, maybe I will see you in a month."

"Sounds great! Thank you, Janice, or should I say Gaelica."

She smiles at me, her eyes soft, "Oh, before you go, I forgot to give you this." She hands me an envelope with a wax seal on the back. "Don't worry about opening it now. Open it when you are ready!"

"Okay," I say hesitantly.

With a smile, she walks away. I tuck the envelope in my sack with my sketchbook and head toward where I'm meeting the other Unnaturals who will drop me off at Earth.

I take one last look around Willorian, taking in everything and smiling. With that, we all jump, transporting us home.

Epilogue

We found three of the twenty dragon scales and plan to find more soon. I personally have discovered the house, and even though I refuse to tell anyone else about it, I know Echo has seen a drawing of it in my sketchbook. I had prepared myself for her questioning the house but had mentally prepared to tell her it was a house here on Earth I liked and wanted to remember. Thankfully, it didn't come to that.

Looking up, I see my apartment building looming over me. I drag my now heavy drawstring bag, filled with sketchbooks I've collected over the past few months, various outfits, and the wax-sealed envelope, and drag it over the threshold of my apartment. I call out for Mom but am only met with silence. I see a note on the fridge along with a twenty-dollar bill.

Aidan,
I got called into work again. I'm sorry. I know we were supposed to order takeout and play board games tonight, but we'll have to do that another time, maybe tomorrow! There's some money for dinner near the flower pot on the counter. Order anything you'd like, even your smelly favorite Indian food. :)
Welcome home, and tomorrow, we'll discuss online school options. Yes, I'd like for you to complete high school.
Enjoy dinner!

```
Love you, Mom.
```

I smile as I read Mom's note. Looking at the money, I decide to order something later. I'm exhausted, and hunger has not called my name yet.

Heading to the couch, I collapse onto its cushions and pull a blanket over my body. Grabbing the remote, I turn on some cartoons. Reflecting on the last few weeks, I start to doze off. My eyelids feel incredibly heavy.

> *"I'm transported back to the first lake where the Elders placed the excess powers into the dragon scales. This time, there's a figure cloaked in dark brown, resembling a medieval cloak with a hood that obscures their face. Fifteen scales float above the lake, vibrating— or perhaps the lake itself is vibrating. The water creates ripples on the surface as though the sound emanates from a large speaker nearby.*
>
> *I hear chanting coming from the figure. Reluctantly, I step forward to get a closer look.*
>
> *With a sharp turn, the figure faces me and shouts, "Where are they? Where are the remaining five? I NEED THEM! I know you know where the HOUSE is! Tell me! Tell me, SON!"*
>
> *I stare back blankly, full of complete shock.*
>
> *"Dad?"*

THE END

Authors Note

Aidan is based on me, at least to some extent. I have dyslexia, and throughout school, I struggled with reading and comprehension. Completing a single homework assignment would take me nearly two hours, and then I would have three more subjects to tackle that night. My usual routine after school was to arrive home around 3:30 p.m., start on one school subject, and either finish it or take a break to switch to another. When my dad came home, we would go outside to care for our livestock, then head back inside to continue with homework. Most nights, I went to bed around 9:30 or 10:00 pm., spending close to four or five hours just doing homework or trying to study. This was my routine from middle school through high school.

I struggled with test anxiety. I had many tutors helping me with Math, English, and ACT prep. I took the ACT close to ten times and only achieved an 18, while most colleges require a 21 or 24 for acceptance. Back then, sharing those results would have scared me, but I have grown past that fear and anxiety. After I graduated high school, my parents and I had me tested for dyslexia, and it turns out that's what I had been struggling with. When I read, my brain added or subtracted letters from the words.

Everyone's brain works in different and mysterious ways. After being diagnosed with dyslexia, I went through the

Davis Dyslexia Program, which helped rewire the brain from dyslexia to a more typical reading pattern. This isn't a cure-all, but it helped me learn to read more efficiently. Most dyslexics can picture objects like trees or cats when thinking of those words, but "it," "and", "then," or "the" are more complex to visualize.

In the program, I learned to take those problematic words, look them up in a dictionary, and create their definitions in a few words, transforming them into objects with clay to form a 3D image for each word. For example, if I read "A large dog is jumping against the tree," I could create a movie-in my head-of a large dog (a Labrador, since that's what I grew up with) jumping against a tree. The "a" describes a single tree, so my brain would picture one tree, probably a maple tree.

In my story, I didn't explicitly state that Aidan has dyslexia because, at his age, I didn't know what kind of learning disability I had, and I wanted to reflect that in my book. Aidan experiences the same anxiety and nervousness I felt when reading aloud or trying to focus on studying.

I have wanted to write a book for a while but never thought I could because of my dyslexia. I admit that I am not great at spelling or grammar, but thanks to my parents, husband, and amazing friends, I could bounce ideas off them, and they helped me through it.

Aidan is similar to me with his undiagnosed dyslexic brain, but he got to experience the magic of an unknown world. Even though we live in the real world, full of responsibilities and hardship, don't let that stop you from finding the magic in the world. Don't let anything hold you back.

www.ingramcontent.com/pod-product-compliance
Lightning Source LLC
Chambersburg PA
CBHW020947310726
48980CB00001B/89

* 9 7 9 8 9 9 2 4 2 5 1 1 6 *